Leo's Arm Came Around Her Possessively, And He Grinned, Showing Off His Perfect, White Teeth.

"Good. You're still here," he said.

"It's my bed. My house," Abby said. "Where would I go?"

"So—are you going to marry me?"

"There are a million logical reasons why that's a very bad idea."

"You're pregnant. If we're unhappy, we'll get a divorce. Big deal."

Big deal? To Abby, it was a *very* big deal.

Dear Reader,

Many of you have written me asking if I intended to write about the missing twins from my GOLDEN SPURS novels, and, yes, I always did.

The Throw-Away Bride is the first twin's story. When Leo Storm, the CEO of the Golden Spurs ranching empire, discovers that Abby Collins, the woman who lives on the ranch next to his, is one of the twins, instead of telling her, he beds her. Ashamed of their passionate night, she scorns him until she discovers she's pregnant. Leo has been down this dark road before, so when she confides in him, he's not about to risk losing his precious child. Thus, he forces her into a marriage of convenience.

When Abby finds out who she really is and the length Leo's gone to in order to keep her identity a secret, she wonders if he married her for the baby or because he's ruthlessly ambitious and wants to be wedded to a member of the legendary family he works for. Does their fragile relationship stand a chance?

Look for her long-missing twin, Becky, and her story in June 2009, from the Silhouette Desire line.

Ann Major

ANN MAJOR

THE THROW-AWAY BRIDE

Published by Silhouette Books

America's Publisher of Contemporary Romance

 SILHOUETTE BOOKS

ISBN-13: 978-0-373-76912-4
ISBN-10:   0-373-76912-1

Recycling programs
for this product may
not exist in your area.

THE THROW-AWAY BRIDE

Copyright © 2008 by Ann Major

Books by Ann Major

Silhouette Desire

Midnight Fantasy #1304
Cowboy Fantasy #1375
A Cowboy & a Gentleman #1477
Shameless #1513
The Bride Tamer #1586
The Amalfi Bride #1784
Sold Into Marriage #1832
Mistress for a Month #1869
*The Throw-Away Bride #1912

MIRA Books

The Girl with the Golden Spurs
The Girl with the Golden Gun
The Secret Lives of Doctors' Wives

*Golden Spurs

ANN MAJOR

lives in Texas with her husband of many years and is the mother of three grown children. She has a master's degree from Texas A&M at Kingsville, Texas, and is a former English teacher. She is a founding board member of Romance Writers of America and a frequent speaker at writers' groups.

Ann loves to write; she considers her ability to do so a gift. Her hobbies include hiking in the mountains, sailing, ocean kayaking, traveling and playing the piano. But most of all she enjoys her family.

I dedicate this book to my late, much-beloved mother,
Ann C. Major, even though I know she was really
a true-blue horror fan.

One

Central Texas, near Austin
Abigail Colins's ranch outside Bastrop, Texas
Early morning, first of June

Predictable Leo Storm had seemed like a safe choice.

When you go to a bar on the rebound intending to dance with a wild cowboy or two, and you end up sleeping with the dullest, safest, most-buttoned-down guy there—your next-door neighbor of all people—you don't expect earth-shattering consequences…in his bed or afterward.

Abigail Collins's eyes burned, and not from mucking out her horse Coco's stall. She was suffering from a bad case of Poor-Me Syndrome.

Greedy, ambitious CEOs like Leo Storm were supposed to play it safe when it came to sex. They were supposed to carry wallets full of condoms and fall asleep after doing it once.

Apparently Leo hadn't read his CEO rule book on said subject. His skill and enthusiastic ardor as a lover had made Abigail's toes tingle and her bones melt. She'd opened herself to him in ways that had caused her to despise herself and blame him the next morning. They'd done it so many times, she'd been tender for days. Needless to say, she'd avoided the heck out of him ever since.

So, the discovery that she was pregnant—by Leo— sucked big-time.

You can have anything you want—as long as you're willing to pay the price, her mother used to say. Trouble was, the price was due, and Abby didn't want to pay.

Ever since she'd found out about her condition last week, she'd been wallowing in self-misery—not that she was proud of such childish behavior.

As soon as she'd gotten up this morning and had finished going to the bathroom, desperation had overwhelmed her again, and she'd flipped the toilet lid down and collapsed on it, sniveling like a baby. A little later she'd had another good cry while knocking her forehead against the wet tiles of her shower.

As if buckets full of tears or regrets—and don't forget whining—did any good. Some things just had to be faced.

Pregnant! By Leo Storm!

She was a control freak and single with no desire for a long-term alliance of any kind after being hurt so badly when her boyfriend, Shanghai Knight, had dumped her.

Since puberty she'd gone for short-term relationships with cowboys like Shanghai; not for boring, bossy, calculating, corporate, money guys without souls like Leo. She'd been the brains, and the cowboys been the brawn.

She licked her lips and wiped the sweat off her brow. Well, she wasn't going to cry again. No use indulging in any more pity parties. She was a big girl—whether she was acting like one or not. She could handle this. She *had* to handle this.

Which was why she was telling Leo today. Surely she'd feel better once that was behind her. She closed her eyes and tried not to think about Leo's white, drawn face and blazing black eyes the last time she'd seen him. He'd been furious at her. Not only furious—he'd said he was through with her.

Usually being in the barn with Coco, her gentle palomino, soothed her. Not today. Not when she dreaded driving into San Antonio and telling a certain stubborn, macho CEO, who was now refusing to take her calls, that *they* had a little problem.

Every time she bent over to scoop another pitchfork load of manure and dirty straw into the wheelbarrow, the zipper of her jeans slid a little lower, reminding her of *their* mutual problem and *that* night, that one night with him that she'd tried so hard to forget.

Not that he'd wanted to forget. He'd made it very clear he'd wanted her—again and again. He was nothing if not determined. He'd called her both at home and at her office. He'd dropped by, but finally when she'd rejected him for about the tenth time, he'd become so angry he'd issued his ultimatum—which she'd ignored.

Having rid himself of her, he wouldn't be happy to

learn that *that* night was now every bit as impossible for her to forget as it had been for him.

Heaving in a breath, she rested her pitchfork against the wheelbarrow and tugged her zipper back up. She was panting by the time she'd managed it, so she didn't even try to snap the waistband. The jeans had been tight when she'd bought them, but since she'd planned to take off a couple of pounds, she hadn't worried about it.

No chance of losing those pounds anytime soon.

As she stooped to pick up the pitchfork, the cell phone in her back pocket vibrated against her hip. She threw the pitchfork back down hard, and it stabbed a mound of hay so violently that Coco, who was just outside the stall, danced backward, her hooves clattering on the concrete floor.

Oh, God, what if her big darling slipped because of her thoughtlessness?

"Easy girl," she whispered, her tone gentle even as the stench of straw and urine and horse in such close quarters caused nausea to roil in her stomach.

She hoped against hope that Leo had relented and was returning her call like a reasonable individual. Maybe he'd even agree to stop by her ranch house tonight to talk. Much as she would dread seeing him, it would be so nice if she could avoid the drive to San Antonio and the humiliation of fighting her way into his office after he'd made it clear he never wanted to see her again.

Not that she could blame him for that. Her heart knocked as she remembered accusing him of not being able to take no for an answer and of stalking her. He'd hissed in a breath. But she'd seen the acute pain in his black eyes right before he'd whirled, pitched the roses he'd brought her into the trash and quietly walked back to his truck. Later he'd called her and had delivered his ultimatum, which, for some weird reason, she'd replayed at least a dozen times in her mind. Did she enjoy suffering or what?

Instead of Leo's name, the number of In the Pink!, Abigail's own company located on a side street just off Congress Avenue in downtown Austin lit up the blue LED of her mobile phone.

Kel, her executive secretary, best friend, unpaid therapist…and of late, her number-one shoulder to cry on, was calling.

Damn.

Abigail sagged against the wall of the barn. A tear rolled down her cheek as she caught her breath. Then she swallowed and squeaked out a hello that she'd meant to sound chirpy.

"Hey, Abby, do you have a cold or something?"

"Or something." Abigail felt frozen. "This thing has me all messed up."

"I know. Hormones."

Or the terror of Leo Storm, of what he would say and do to her this morning at her news, especially after the way she'd treated him.

"Other than feeling like I'm about to have a nervous breakdown, I'm fine. Never better." Somehow she managed a hollow laugh. "As fine as someone with morning sickness can be, mucking out a stall…before they face a firing squad."

"You need to hire somebody for that yucky-mucky stuff now."

A city girl through and through, Kel didn't get horses.

"I know. You're right. I will."

"So, anything I need to know before I start scheduling your day?"

"Yes. I-I'm going to tell him…today."

"Oh? When exactly?"

"This morning! First thing!"

"Wow. Well, finally!"

"Putting it off is driving me crazy. The only problem is it looks like I'm going to have to track him down. He won't return my calls."

"You should have listened to your smart secretary. Didn't I tell you, you should call him and apologize—"

"Smart-assed secretary!"

"Big-assed, too." Kel laughed. "And getting bigger. Jan brought in two dozen donuts this morning coated with yummy strawberry goo. I'm inhaling my second."

"Okay. Well, I didn't call him back or apologize. And ever since, he's avoided the ranch and me. Now he won't even take my calls or call me back."

"Why are we surprised?"

"I said it was urgent. I've left several messages with his secretary, too. Yesterday, she actually got snappy and said he had no intention of returning my calls. I can't tell you how humiliating that was. I'm not about to tell a witch like her to tell him I'm pregnant with his child, so I guess I have to drive over there."

"Right. You think you'll get back here this afternoon?"

"After lunch. I'll probably be a basket case after seeing him."

"Do you want me to cancel your afternoon?"

"No!"

"Is there anything I can do?" Kel's voice was soft with concern.

"Just be your smart-assed self and put out any and all home fires."

"Don't worry about us," Kel said. "Just take care of you."

They hung up.

Abigail's hands began to shake again as she slid her phone in her back pocket. Compulsively, she began marching back and forth in the barn, straightening tack that didn't need to be straightened, lining up bottles and brushes on shelves, trying to feel she controlled something. She got a broom and began to sweep the feed that Coco had shaken out of the feed sack when she'd grabbed it by her teeth earlier.

Coco walked up and lowered her head almost apologetically. It was her way of begging for her favorite treat, a mixture of oats and molasses.

"Not today, big girl. Not after this big mess you made!"

Setting the broom against the wall, Abby pushed the wheelbarrow full of dirty straw outside the barn and up a small hill where she dumped it before heading toward the house. Coco, who adored her, trailed behind her in the hope of being stroked or fed, but Abby was too distracted to notice her as she usually did.

Pregnant! By Leo….

Even though Abigail had taken the pregnancy tests a week ago—three of them—she still couldn't believe she was in this mess. She was a businesswoman, an entrepreneur with a staff of forty, the owner of her own ranch. Make that a ranchette. But still…she was *la capitana* of her ship! Even if she'd sailed headlong into the rocks.

She reached into her pocket and pulled out her phone. Quickly she scrolled down to Leo's cell number and punched it. Once again she listened to it ring until his voice mail picked up. So, he still refused to answer. She flipped her phone shut and began to pace.

So what else was new? She'd watched him screen his calls, so it was easy to imagine his black eyes grimly eyeing her name before his jaw tightened and he thrust his buzzing phone back in his pocket.

How eager he'd been for her to call him just two weeks ago…until she'd accused him of stalking her. He'd stormed home, but had called her back. She hadn't answered, but he'd left a message.

"Stalking? Is that what you think? I thought you were just embarrassed and wary because we sort of took our relationship too far and too fast that first night," he'd said. "I was hoping I could convince you that I think you're great, as a person I mean. That I was willing to slow things down. But if you really want me to leave you the hell alone, I will. Call me back today, or I'm through, and I mean through."

She didn't know him very well, but she imagined he was probably a man who meant what he said.

She clenched her fist. It was ridiculous how crushed she felt that he wouldn't return her calls now. She'd told herself all he'd wanted was more wild, uninhibited sex. Had she taken the intensity of his interest for granted? Had he meant more to her than she'd known?

In any case, when she hadn't done exactly what he'd wanted, he'd quickly thrown her away. Like her mother and her father had…after Becky, her twin, had vanished. Abigail killed that thought. She didn't like to think about her long-missing twin or that she herself had never mattered very much to anybody.

She drew in a sharp breath. Yesterday after calling his secretary, she'd tucked Leo's business card in her dresser under her lingerie. Fisting her hands at her sides, she marched toward her house. She had to find that card again and call his office. Then she'd punch his exact address into her GPS and drive there.

Letting her screen door bang behind her, she rushed inside her kitchen and washed her hands before heading toward her bedroom.

She took her time at the faucet. Why had she let him pick her up that night in that bar? Why had she gone to that bar when she'd felt so lonely and rejected and vulnerable after Shanghai had dumped her for Mia Kemble?

Why had she thrown herself at Shanghai, a wild-bull rider who'd never been particularly fascinated with her in the first place?

It was no use asking questions like that. She had to go from here. She'd been hurting, so she'd had a night of wild sex with Leo Storm. As a result, the next pair of jeans she bought would have an elastic waistband.

Had he even used a condom? She wasn't sure. Except for a few shamefully sizzling memories, the night was a horrible blur.

Once inside her bedroom, she yanked the top drawer of her dresser open and began ransacking her underwear. When his card wasn't there, she looked up and caught a glimpse of a pale, thin woman with guilt-shadowed eyes and clumps of butterscotch tangles falling about her shoulders. She stood up straighter and sucked in her stomach.

Even though her jeans wouldn't snap, her tummy didn't look the least bit fat…*yet*. Still, thoughts of her future big belly panicked her.

Oh, God. Pretty soon she'd have to tell her staff. Shaking even harder, she squeezed her lashes shut and then yanked the second drawer open so hard it fell to the oak floor. She knelt and began clawing through her nightgowns and T-shirts.

Never again did she want a repeat of a week like the last one. After a visit to her doctor, Abigail had realized that she couldn't go through this alone…or end it as Kel had suggested. So, if Leo thought he could play Mr. CEO jerk and just give her that ultimatum and then walk away…the way everybody in her life had always walked away…well…at least, she'd tell him off first.

A final image of her mother packing her suitcase and telling her she was leaving her father—and leaving her—made her heart ache as she opened a third drawer.

Abby didn't know much about babies, but she knew enough to know her baby would want her to at least tell its father about the pregnancy.

She suspected that Leo had been staying in San Antonio and avoiding his ranch. Or rather the Little Spur, the ranch he owned with his brother, Connor, which was next door to hers and to Shanghai's Buckaroo Ranch. She hadn't seen him or his black truck—not once at the Little Spur—since his ultimatum, and lately she'd been watching. *Well, too bad, Mr. Rich Know-It-All, Macho CEO! You should have kept your pants zipped.*

The last thing she wanted to think about was that night in the bar after they'd danced dirty and she'd become as intensely aroused as he'd been. He'd kissed her, a second time, his tongue in her mouth, his hands sliding all over her, caressing, cupping, possessing. She'd melted, utterly melted like a slab of rich chocolate too near a flame.

Later in his loft in downtown San Antonio, she'd climbed onto his dining-room table and stripped. The next morning when she'd awakened next to his tanned, naked body, all she'd wanted was to run from him and forget.

She dreaded facing him again. He'd probably suggest the modern options just as Kel had.

"So, why even tell him?" Kel had said. "Just take care of it. In a week you'll forget it ever happened."

"You don't have my memories, Kel."

Some things, one never forgets.

Abigail hadn't ever told her about that fatal afternoon two identical eight-year-old little girls had run up a twisting trail after a wild turkey in the Franklin Mountains. The sun had been setting. The thin, impish face of her twin, Becky, had been rosily alight, her hair backlit with fire.

"Wait!" Becky had screamed. "Wait for me!"

Abigail had yelled back. "No! Come on!" Then she'd turned, expecting her twin to follow as she always did. But that had been the last time she'd ever seen her sister.

Abby opened the last drawer. She still dreamed about Becky, and now she dreamed about her baby, too. She'd never wanted to be part of a family again and open herself up for more hurt, so being pregnant was very risky for her. Still, she wasn't about to throw away her precious unborn baby. Not when she knew how sacred family was if you were lucky enough to have it and how easy it was to make irrevocable mistakes.

Don't think about Becky.

Abigail's hand closed around a card. Not Leo's card, but a Christmas card…from her father.

The money, fifty dollars in cash that he'd carelessly tossed in the envelope as a last-minute gift, was still inside it. Not that he'd spent Christmas with her. His only gift had been the card with that single bill, and it had arrived two weeks late, long after she'd given up hope he'd even thought of her at Christmas.

For a fleeting second she remembered that last Christmas before Becky had disappeared. She and her twin had conspired to make sure their parents didn't know they no longer believed in Santa Claus. They'd made cookies for Santa and set out small pink teacups filled with milk near the fireplace.

A dark feeling of loneliness washing over her, she hugged her tummy. When she'd been a little girl, she'd never felt alone. She'd had a twin, someone to share everything with. They'd both taken ballet and had had identical pink tutus and tights.

Don't think about Becky.

Abby was shaking as she tucked the Christmas card back under her sweaters. She smoothed the dark blond tangles out of her eyes. One thing she knew—no matter what Leo did, she intended to love her baby with all her heart. Bad as things seemed right now, maybe this was her second chance.

Finally, her hand closed numbly on Leo's expensive, engraved card. Lifting it, she stared at his name in bold black type. Dreading his condescending baritone, she swallowed hard, grabbed her cell and punched in his office number before her fear could escalate.

"Golden Spurs. Leo Storm's office. Miriam Jones. How can I help you?" The crisp, no-nonsense voice that had so annoyed her yesterday was as impersonal as ever.

"I need to see Mr. Storm. This morning. It's urgent."

"Mr. Storm makes his own appointments, and I assure you, he makes as few as possible. He's quite busy today. Perhaps you could send him an e-mail and outline the reasons why you need a meeting."

"N-no...no e-mail!"

"Your name please?"

She gave it—as she had yesterday. There was a long pause. Then his snoop of a secretary asked more questions before excusing herself to confer with Leo. The woman's voice, chillier than ever, came back on the phone almost immediately. The nosy witch was nothing if not efficient.

"He says he can't see you, and that you'll know the reason why."

"What? Did you say it was urgent?"

"Yes. Just like I did yesterday." Another long pause so this could sink in. "Is there anything else I can help you with, Miss Collins?" the impossible woman asked, her chilly tone holding polite finality.

"Did you really tell him it was urgent?"

The next thing Abigail knew, the woman had said a dismissive goodbye and Abby was listening to a dial tone.

Her heart pounding, Abby punched redial. "When is the best time this morning for me to see him?" she blurted before his secretary could say anything.

"I told you what Mr. Storm said—"

"You don't understand. He doesn't understand. I *have* to see him. Work me in."

"That could take hours. And even then, I can't promise—"

"Just do it!"

"He's been down in South Texas at the Golden Spurs for the last four days. I'm afraid he has a lot to catch up on. And…I'm afraid he was most emphatic about not wanting—"

Abigail snapped her phone shut. Scooping up a handful of clothes off the floor, grabbing a pair of heels, she stomped into her bathroom. Five minutes later, she looked more or less presentable with her hair in a tight coil at her nape and her body clad in a pair of black slacks and a blue knit top. Slinging her black jacket over one arm and her purse over the other, she barged out her front door and raced toward her white Lincoln.

Coco looked up and whinnied expectantly, but Abby marched past her.

She had to tell Leo her news—whether or not he wanted to hear it.

She hoped she ruined his day, his week, the rest of his life—just like he'd ruined hers.

Two

Immense paintings and photographs of the world-famous Golden Spurs Ranch, which was two hundred miles south of San Antonio, decorated two walls of Leo Storm's impressive outer offices. Sheets of glass along another wall looked out over the winding San Antonio River fringed darkly by cypress trees and buildings. Not that Abby was impressed by his showy office or the dramatic view as she scribbled a note to Leo and folded it again and again until it was a tiny wad.

If she'd been agitated when she'd walked in, she was totally charged after sitting here an hour, watching his secretary pointedly ignore her and escort others who'd come in after her, in to see him, the last of whom had been an elderly, unhappy-looking rancher.

She tried and failed to distract herself by studying his office. The massive photographs were of cowboys, oil wells, cattle drives and the legendary big house where the Kemble family he worked for had entertained presidents and kings, and lately, Arab sheiks. She'd been there— once. The museum-quality, nineteenth century oil paintings were mostly scenes of cowboys and Native Americans, although there was the inevitable clichéd landscape of Texas hill country, live oaks and bluebonnets.

The opulence and grandeur of the Golden Spurs headquarters were meant to impress, but Abigail merely felt incensed as she continued to languish in a huge red leather chair that dwarfed her.

Impatiently, Abigail looked at his secretary again. Naturally, the tight-lipped, string bean of a redhead with that awful knot screwed at the top of her head rustled papers and pretended to ignore her in that arrogant way waitresses in posh restaurants do when you need silverware and wave madly while trying to signal them.

Abigail glanced at her watch and then up at the photograph of the big house again. She'd been there once and did not have fond memories of it.

Damn his hide! Leo owed her. He'd ruined her life, hadn't he? She was through playing his games! She looked at her watch. If she didn't do something, Leo would never see her.

Getting up from the chair, she rushed up to his secretary's desk to plead her case for what had to be the fourth or fifth time.

Her forehead puckering, the redhead, who was clearly losing patience, pursed her mouth. "Yes, Miss Collins?"

"Would you give him this note—*please?*"

Arching her brows, the woman narrowed her eyes as she studied the tightly folded wad. Finally she took it, rolled her chair back and got up without a word. Abigail watched her walk briskly down a long, wide hall and open his door. A few minutes later she repeated that stiff-legged march, her heels clicking all the way back to her desk. Then she spun her chair and sat down.

"Well?" Abby said.

The woman shook her head. "Mr. Storm says he's very sorry, but he's busy—*all day*. I tried to tell you that you'd be wasting your time, that you'd be better off sending him an e-mail. He told me to remind you that you made the decision to break off your relationship with him."

What? He was blaming her and humiliating her at the same moment?

Rage and embarrassment sent fire blazing through Abby. How dare he deliberately humiliate her?

Relationship? Since when did they have a relationship?

Somehow she resisted the impulse to scream. "I have to see him," she repeated softly. "It's important."

"I'm sorry."

Clearly, she wasn't. She'd probably read some manual that told her never to meet anger with anger. Embarrassed for Abby, the woman stared down at her desk.

"I've told you repeatedly this is urgent."

"And I've told you he said he can't see you."

Abigail could feel herself hurtling toward some edge. She knew she had to get a grip. "Oh, really? Can't or won't?"

Behind her, she heard heavy footsteps. When she turned, two large, beefy men in dark suits were heading toward her. They looked like cops. Their purposeful gazes and tread both energized and terrified her.

His secretary followed her gaze. "I'm truly sorry, but he said he wants you out of the building. I'm afraid he called security. They'll escort—"

"Damn him!" Abigail barged past the impossible woman and raced down the hall toward Leo's office.

The men shouted her name and then thundered after her. His secretary cried, "Wait! You can't go in there!"

Just you watch me!

Abigail banged his door open, walked inside and slammed it so hard pins flew out of her hair and sprinkled onto Leo's polished oak floor.

"Maybe a lot of people admire you because you're the CEO of Golden Spurs, but I know you too well. You're a ruthless, cold-hearted bastard." Mike Ransom had to yell to make himself heard over the raised voices behind the door.

Leo's focus was on Abby's voice, too, and he grew angry that just knowing she was out there could rattle him. Security must have arrived to handle Abby, but it didn't sound like his men were succeeding. She'd made it crystal clear she dated cowboys—only cowboys and only short-term. That she disliked him, that she thought his type serious, dull and greedy. So what the hell did she want with him now?

"I work with dull city guys like you all day long, men who don't ever think about anything but making money," she'd told him at one point. "I don't want to play with them at night when I'm looking for a little excitement."

Why the hell had she broken her sacred rule then and slept with him?

More importantly, why the hell had he broken his

own sacred rule—which was never to combine business with sex? Dammit, the Golden Spurs board had hired him to find the late Caesar Kemble's missing twin daughter. He in turn had hired his brother, Connor, a security specialist, to look for her. Connor had stunned him when he'd informed him that their own neighbor, Abigail Collins, and her missing twin were probably the Golden Spurs heiresses.

Leo had tracked Abigail to that bar that night to obtain a DNA sample from her, not to bed her. The beer bottle he'd bagged proved she was a Kemble.

With immense effort he forced himself to concentrate on Mike Ransom. The old man looked frail and weathered. Despite his blustering, his thin shoulders were slumped in defeat, the fabric of his jacket hanging against his body like a broken bat's wings.

The snap and toughness damn sure hadn't gone out of the old man, and Leo suppressed twinges of admiration and sympathy. "If I'm a bastard, the world has you to thank."

"I wouldn't sell the Running R. Not for twice your offer. And never to you."

"You don't have a choice. Just like I didn't have a choice when you kicked me the hell off the Running R for getting Nancy pregnant when I was eighteen and didn't have a dime to my name. How does it feel to know you're helpless and at *my* mercy now?"

Strangely, Leo didn't feel nearly as happy as he'd thought he would now that he'd turned the tables on the old man.

The ruckus Abby was stirring up outside was growing louder. Not good.

Leo longed to storm past Mike and deal with Abigail himself but forced himself to remain at his desk.

"This is revenge, pure and simple," Ransom said, still glowering at him.

"You would know," Leo replied.

"You don't even want the ranch. You're just after it because you know I love it and want Cal and Nancy to inherit it someday…and because you've never gotten over…."

No, he hadn't gotten over his pregnant girlfriend, Nancy, refusing to marry him because he was broke and homeless. No, he hadn't gotten over Nancy marrying Ransom's son, Cal, instead. No, he hadn't gotten over losing his daughter. Not when he knew Ransom had caused all these things.

"Think what you like…."

Leo would have said more. He'd waited years for this day. He'd been psyched to finish Ransom off this morning in a cool, bloodless business battle of wills.

Suddenly he heard racing footsteps. His door opened and slammed. He shot to his feet just as Abigail locked herself inside his inner sanctum and whirled on him, her dark, gold hair tumbling over her shoulders like a silk curtain.

"Get out!" Leo yelled even as the memory of his hands in her hair as he held her close so he could kiss her came back to him. The memory made heat pulse through him.

Frozen, she stared at him with the wide, frightened eyes of a doe caught in his sights as she tried to smooth her wild hair. Her face was worrisomely thin and much too pale.

He remembered how her eyes had blazed after their

first kiss, her pupils dilating with passion that night. Now dark blue circles shadowed her lovely hazel eyes. Except for the bold blue of her knit top and all that butterscotch hair falling over her shoulders in such wild disarray, she was dressed as primly as a schoolteacher in a black jacket and slacks.

She stooped and retrieved several pins from the floor. Pulling her hair back, she secured it again, so that she looked much more severe. He remembered how sexily she'd been dressed in the bar that night. Still, despite Ransom's raised eyebrows and her attempt to look all prim and proper, her haunted, condemning gaze both burned him and drew him. He felt his body harden and heat even as Ransom's cold eyes drilled him.

Hell. He had to get rid of her. She'd made it abundantly clear that she considered sex with him a huge mistake and that she despised him and his type intensely and not just for seducing her, as she'd put it—which was a laugh if ever there was one.

Ever since she'd slipped from his arms and run away without a goodbye, she'd been telling him to go to hell in various ways. But she'd been as eager for it as he'd been. Then she'd had the gall to tell him she'd been pretending he was Shanghai that night. The final straw had been when she'd accused him of stalking her. Damn her, he was through.

He wasn't about to admit that that night had opened doors into his heart that had been closed since Nancy, Cal and Mike Ransom had ruined his life when he'd been little more than a kid.

"I'm busy," he said. "You're interrupting an important meeting."

"Believe me, I don't want to see you, either! But like I told your secretary, this is urgent! And, Leo, I swear— it won't take long," she whispered in a voice that cracked. "I've got to talk to you. After you hear me out, you don't have to see me again."

I don't want to see you, either. Both those words and her raw, hateful tone cut, but her shadowed eyes were scaring the hell out of him. What was wrong?

With an effort, he fought his concern and curiosity and kept his gaze and voice hard. "As you can see, I'm busy."

"Not anymore you're not. I'm just leaving," Ransom growled. "The bastard's all yours, sweetheart. Enjoy." His last word seething with sarcasm, Ransom shot him a murderous look before pivoting. Unlocking and opening the door, he slammed it behind him.

Seeing their chance, the two security officers rushed the door, but Abigail was faster. Swiftly, she shot the bolt. When the officers banged on the door, she leaned against it, her mouth trembling.

Her face was ashen, and the lack of brilliance in her wide eyes was beginning to frighten him. She was scared to death of him. She swallowed, or, at least, she tried to.

Gagging, she gave a little cry. Then, cupping one hand over her mouth, she lurched toward his desk. Was she seriously ill?

Fear gripped him even as her eyes grew even wider in panic. With her hand still covering her mouth and the other crossed over her stomach, she sank to her knees and retched violently. For another long minute she made horrible, dry-heaving sounds as she held on to his wastebasket.

"What the hell is wrong with you?"

Finally, when she lifted her desperate gaze to his, her hair wild again as it fell over her shoulders, he saw Nancy's white, terrified face from the past.

"Can't you guess?" Abby whispered.

And he knew.

Still, he had to ask her. "Morning sickness?" he muttered, hoping to hell and back he was wrong.

When she nodded, the stark pain in her mute eyes tore off a corner of his soul. Shuddering, he shut his eyes and took a deep breath, attempting to clear his head. Not that the trick worked. The air suddenly felt too thick to breathe. Or maybe his heart was thudding too violently.

"You'd better not be trying to nail me for somebody else's kid…for Shanghai's…"

She blushed, and when a single tear slid down her cheek, he bit his tongue so hard he tasted blood.

"I hate you," she whispered. "I think you're… you're horrible."

God, she was right. How could he have said that? He was the worst creep on the planet.

When she spoke again, her eyes flashed with real hatred and her voice had sharpened. "But it's yours. I wish it wasn't, believe me. I never wanted to see you again, either!"

Her barbs stung. "You would have preferred Shanghai! Even if he is married. You made that abundantly clear."

She ignored his comment. "There are tests that will prove it's yours…if you don't believe me. There's DNA."

He felt his neck heat guiltily. He knew way too much about DNA.

"That won't be necessary," Leo said through clenched teeth. "Look, I'm sorry…."

"Relax. You don't have to apologize. I hate you just as much as you dislike me."

"Right." No surprise that she didn't want his child any more than she'd wanted him.

He ran his hand through his hair, staring at her for a long moment while her eyes damned him to hell and back. When she knew the whole truth—why he'd been in the bar that night—she'd have even more justification for hating him. If the Golden Spurs board learned the truth, this could spell the end of his career.

Abruptly, Leo strode across his office and opened the door that led to his private washroom. He turned on the faucet and dampened a towel with cold water. He poured water into a glass. When he returned, he handed the towel and the glass of water to her.

"Sit down before you fall. Bathe your face, and we'll figure out what the hell you need to do next."

"I need to do? It's yours, too," she repeated dully.

"Right. I get that."

"But you didn't believe—"

"I said I get it—okay? It's mine. Unpleasant realities have a way of sinking in fast. Now this is what we're going to do—"

"You can't just boss me around. I don't work for you."

"You're carrying my child."

"You're supposed to be smart! Did you even use a condom?" she accused.

"Yes, dammit. Several."

She flushed as if it embarrassed her to remember once hadn't been enough for either of them.

"I wasn't some kid, in such a rush and so madly in love, that I didn't think…."

He'd done that once, years ago with Nancy when he'd been eighteen. Still, that aside, he'd been wild for her. He hadn't just happened to go to that bar. He'd known she'd be there. He'd had something very important to tell her.

Something very important to get from her.

Too bad for them both that she'd dressed so sexily and had looked so sad that he'd let himself get derailed before he'd obtained what he'd needed.

He remembered how many times they'd done it, and how every time it had just gotten better and better. How she'd moaned and sobbed and opened herself utterly, clinging to him with her legs and arms until he'd hardened again while still inside of her. He'd felt sexy and big and powerful.

He remembered her taking him between her lips, kissing him until he'd felt himself in a hot swirl of soft, wet satin and had climaxed in her mouth. She'd been sweet, hot and good. He'd been on a high for several weeks after that night. He'd been unable to believe that she would want to throw him and what they'd had that night—which had been that mind-altering, at least for him—away.

As if she read his mind, color flooded her face. "I—I don't remember much about that night."

"Right. Lucky you. I wish I could forget you and all that happened between us as easily."

"Well, I'll have the baby now as a constant reminder."

"So you want to keep it?" His rush of relief stunned him.

She sprang out of her chair, sputtering at him angrily. "D-don't you even dare suggest anything else the way Kel did, or I'll…or…."

"Hey…hey… Calm down." He rushed to her and placed his hands on her shoulders.

At his touch, something raw and true sparked in her eyes. Then hatred followed in its wake.

Heat flashed through every nerve ending in his body. As if burned, she jumped back, and as always he felt stung by her rejection.

Impossible relationships with women. Were they his specialty or what? But this was worse—because it involved his career. He was screwed on every level by this turn of events. Dammit, he liked being CEO of the Golden Spurs, and if he didn't think fast, his career was charred toast.

"Settle down," he muttered, but his voice was deliberately gentle now. "I-I'm glad you want my baby."

"Your baby?" she repeated, backing even farther away from his blunt, broad hands.

When he nodded, relief flooded her face. He fought the softening he felt as she sank slowly back into her chair. He had to remember she was dangerous, exceedingly dangerous on many levels.

He went to his own chair, and she sat in hers staring across his desk at him as if she were in a daze.

"What are we going to do?" she finally whispered. "This is such a shock."

It sure as hell was, and it was far more complex than she knew. He would have to act before she figured out that she held all the trump cards.

"You've had more time to get used to the idea than I have. I'm sure my secretary told you I've got a really jammed schedule today. Why don't I come over tonight? Say around seven? And we'll talk about options."

"I—I would really prefer to meet you in some public place."

"At night? Then you'd have to drive back to your ranch alone. Are you more afraid of me than of some stranger who might follow you home?"

"You don't have to worry about me. I'm used to living alone, to driving home alone."

"If you're having my baby, you and the baby are my responsibility now."

She bristled. As he stared at her narrowed brows, he could almost see a dozen arguments buzzing in that micromanaging brain of hers.

"Okay, forget I said that. I don't want to argue. But are you afraid of me?"

She shook her head furiously.

"Okay, why didn't you want to see me again?"

"I didn't want to see you again because you're pushy and arrogant, and because you're not the kind of man I like."

"Right. You prefer bull riders. Shanghai Knight in particular."

Why was he repeating himself? Because knowing that hurt, dammit. "You pretended I was him, and you wish this was his kid."

She wouldn't meet his gaze. "At least I didn't lie to you about him."

"Didn't you?"

Shanghai. Leo was sick to death of hearing about the guy. Goaded, hardly knowing what he was doing, he leapt out of his chair.

She jumped up, too, but he clamped his hands around her arms and pulled her to him before she could run. The heat of her body nestling against his torso and legs reminded him of her wet, enticing silkiness that night and why he'd been unable to stick to his original agenda in the bar. Hell, she'd filled him with a hunger it might take a lifetime to satisfy.

"Why are you so afraid of me? Did I hurt you? Have I ever hurt you? Forced you?"

He'd done worse than that by getting that DNA sample without telling her, by not informing her who she was. There was no telling what she'd do when she found out. But it was better to kill one snake at a time. He had to know what she thought of him.

"No, but—"

"Yet you called me a stalker…."

She was shaking as he tightened his grip.

She felt good. So damn good. She smelled of wind and trees, of wildflowers.

"I only said that so you'd leave me alone."

"All that Shanghai crap… Are you really in love with him? Or were you just throwing him at me because you couldn't face me after what we'd done?"

She didn't answer, but something in him relaxed a little.

He'd sensed her inner demons right from the beginning. He knew all about inner demons, and like a fool, he'd sympathized.

He should let her go now, but he couldn't. "If you didn't want me, then why did you make love to me again and again that night?"

"I don't know. I can't remember."

"Can't? Or don't want to remember? Do you really hate me the way you said?"

"Y-yes."

"Go on."

Fixing him with her huge, hazel eyes, she tried to form the words but couldn't.

Suddenly he noticed her heart beating in her throat as she swallowed convulsively. Did she want him... just a little? He remembered burying his face in her breasts. How soft she'd been. How sweet she'd tasted when he'd licked each nipple. How eagerly she'd kissed him back.

"Okay, so maybe you don't totally hate me. But we're still in a helluva mess, aren't we?" he said.

Cursing, he ripped off his glasses and crushed her mouth beneath his. Again, she tasted exquisite...like honey. He expected more fight, but like a terrified animal that had exhausted itself after being caught in a trap, she went absolutely still. Finally, when he didn't release her, when the heat of his body seeped into hers, she grasped his muscular shoulders and pressed her soft lips closer to his, opening them to him.

He loosened his grip. Not even then did she run. Slowly her tongue slid against his, mating with his, and she pushed herself tightly against his body. She didn't draw back, not even when she discovered that he was fully aroused. When he pushed himself against her, she caught her breath.

Moaning, arching her pelvis against his erection in bold invitation, she circled his neck and then caressed his cheeks with her hands, framing his face in her palms as she kissed his mouth again and again.

Instantly the sweetness and the passion and the primal perfection of that night she'd spent in his bed flooded him, and everything made sense again. No wonder he'd been unable to believe she didn't want him. No wonder he'd gone back again and again only to endure more painful rejections.

Her response to his kiss and his male arousal was instantaneous and instinctive and true—unlike the negative garbage she'd been dishing out ever since. He wanted this woman.

When he realized how acute and complex his need for her was, and what a terrible, complicated mess he was in, he jerked his mouth from hers and backed a safe distance away. As if there were a safe distance.

His breathing was hard and labored, but so was hers. Maybe she was pregnant, but he was equally trapped.

"Seven o'clock," he muttered, his tone low and fierce. "Your house. If you prefer to be in a public place, I'll drive you into town in my truck."

"You have no right to just take charge."

"Like I already said, you're having my baby. I think that gives me certain rights."

"This—and what just happened—is exactly why I didn't want to tell you. You'll take advantage…."

Hell. She'd liked it—every bit as much as he had.

"But you did tell me. So, I'll see you at seven. Unless you want me to finish what that kiss started…here on my couch."

Her eyes widened as she stared past him to his long, leather couch. Involuntarily, she touched her lower lip with a fingertip in a way that caused desire to pulse in his blood. "No…."

She must have seen the heat in his eyes that signaled how close he was to the edge because she turned and stumbled toward the doors. Twisting the knob, she seemed to panic when the door wouldn't open and began to beat against the wood with her fists.

He walked across the room. Without touching her, he turned the appropriate lock.

"Seven o'clock sharp," he murmured dryly against her ear before she jumped and ran through the open doors, past his secretary and the still-waiting security guards. Leo motioned for them to let her pass.

Watching her slim hips encased in black silk swing back and forth as she disappeared down the hall, he broke out in a sweat. He had to quit lusting after her and think. All hell would damn sure break loose when she and the board discovered who she really was—which meant it was time to consider damage control.

He shut the doors, went to his desk, punched a button and told Miriam to reschedule his late-afternoon appointments.

Sinking into the chair, Leo's mind flashed back to the afternoon his brother, Connor, had barged into his office and tossed his Stetson and several 8 x 10 pictures onto his desk of their cute neighbor from the ranch next to theirs, riding her palomino bareback.

"I'm pretty sure Abby's one of your missing twins, but we need a DNA sample to confirm it," Connor had said.

"Abby?"

"Like I said, we won't know for sure until you obtain the DNA sample."

"Me? You're the hotshot security specialist."

It hadn't taken Connor long to convince him that all he had to do was buy her a cup of coffee and bag her cup.

Leo called her office late one evening to make an appointment and had told her secretary he was Abby's neighbor. In passing, Kel had mentioned where Abby and she were going that night. He'd shown up at the bar and had taken it from there.

A week after Leo had slept with Abby, Connor had called and said they had a DNA match. Abigail was one of the missing Golden Spurs heiresses. Which made her long-vanished twin, Becky, the other one.

Abigail was the last woman he should have slept with. If he didn't figure out a way to turn this new disaster to his advantage, her pregnancy could cost him everything.

Three

Leo sat down in front of his computer, adjusted his webcam and moved his mouse. He was a firm believer in the theory that when the shit hits the fan, the best defense is almost always a good offense.

So, whose ass better to kick than his baby brother's?

Several mouse clicks later, Connor's square-jawed face and broad shoulders filled Leo's screen. They both nodded and said hello. Then Connor, who was obviously having a better day than he was, leaned back in his chair and flashed his trademark lady-killer smile.

"How can I help you, big brother?"

Connor swept a lock of blond hair out of his blue eyes. He'd put in quite a bit of hard time playing the baby brother from hell and wasn't always as easygoing as his present-day smile might indicate. Baby brother had definitely shown his dark side on more than one occasion.

Leo, who'd raised him after Mike Ransom had kicked them both off the Running R Ranch—not that Connor had been to blame for that—had bailed his baby brother out of plenty of messy jams before a nasty altercation with the police had finally convinced Connor to stay on the right side of the law. Connor had joined the Marines, served in Afghanistan, married and had been widowed.

Leo cut to the chase. "So why the hell don't you have any promising leads on Becky Collins? You been sitting on your thumbs or what?"

Connor loosened the knot of his tie and shifted in his leather chair. Not that his cocky, lady-killer smile wavered. "I have my top agent on the case, but so far…nothing. It's as if she vanished into thin air out there in that El Paso park. Hey, ever since I sent you the DNA report that confirms who our sexy neighbor really is, I've been waiting to hear from you. How'd she take it when you told her who she is?"

Counter-kick-in-the-ass. Baby brothers were good at that, especially baby brothers who'd grown up to be talented P.I.'s and in addition owned a large, multifaceted security business with branches in several major Texas cities. Hell, it could be argued that Connor was even more successful than he was. Not something Leo, who was as competitive as hell, liked to think about much.

"I haven't," Leo hedged testily. "Not yet."

"It's been weeks since I found her. A week since I sent the DNA results. What the hell are you waiting for?"

Maybe Connor was sitting in his office in Houston, but the gaze of his big blue eyes shaded by dense black lashes felt as hot as a laser beam.

"It's complicated." *And getting more complicated.*

"You were as excited as hell when I gave you the file on her."

"Yeah, I was."

"You said if the DNA proved I was right, you were going to tell her first thing."

"I intended to." Leo frowned, not liking the interrogation. "When I met her that night, she was still on the rebound because Shanghai, our neighbor, had dumped her to marry Mia Kemble."

"Right, Mia Kemble of the Golden Spurs Ranch; her famous half-sister, or is it cousin?

"Cousin. Only Abby doesn't know who she really is."

"My point. So why don't you tell her?"

He'd been trying to when she'd accused him of stalking her.

"She was pretty vulnerable that night…and in a sort of self-destructive mood. She was acting crazy, and I got crazy. Things got personal pretty quick."

"Usually you put business before pleasure."

"Too bad I didn't that night."

"Tell me you didn't sleep with her."

"I didn't sleep with her," Leo repeated as if by rote. He probably could have fooled anybody but Connor. Connor had an uncanny knack for smelling out a lie.

Connor's smile changed into something more dangerous, and he leaned forward. "Don't just repeat what I said like a damn idiot. Say it like you mean it."

"I wish I could. Hell. Look, she didn't agree to that DNA sample I sent you. Worse, she's pregnant. I'm meeting her tonight to figure out where we go from here."

Connor whistled. "You knocked up the long-missing

secret Golden Spurs heiress you hired my agency to find? How will the Golden Spurs board react to that?"

"Favorably—if I figure out how to make this work for me…."

"Leo! Don't work it! Not this time! Just keep it simple."

Leo didn't say anything.

"Leo! You'd better listen to me. For once, keep your damned ambition in check and just tell her and the board the truth. This is your kid. You don't want to mess things up the way you did last time."

"The way I did? Have you forgotten how Mike Ransom and Cal threw both of us off the Running R when Nancy turned up pregnant, probably because they'd always wanted Nancy's family's ranch? How they convinced her to marry Cal instead of me because they could do so much more for the baby? For little Julie," he amended softly. He swallowed as he remembered Julie, his dark-eyed daughter, a defiant teenager now, a slim woman-child he barely knew, who hated him.

"No, I haven't forgotten, but you don't want that to happen this time, do you? Look, I know what you've been through. But I know these kinds of situations, too. People make incredible messes when they keep secrets or cover shit like this up. Things spin out of control."

"I'm not going to promise you anything. You know as well as I do that honesty got me into a helluva lot of trouble. So much trouble I lost everything. Nancy… Julie… And you—nearly. I used to think I'd never see myself clear."

"It wasn't your fault I went a little wild after Mother died, when it was just the two of us and you were working all the time."

"Maybe it was. I should have paid more attention to you. I shouldn't have let Cal adopt Julie. I should have fought harder be a part of my daughter's life."

"You've gotta forget…like I have."

"You're not me, little brother. If Ransom hadn't thrown me off the Running R…and cut off my college money, then maybe Nancy wouldn't have left me for Cal. I can't forget that."

"Right. Praise the Lord. You're swimming in success, and you still want that old man's head on a spike."

"You know something funny—Mike Ransom was in my office today. I had the bastard in the palm of my hand, but instead of squeezing, I let him walk out the door."

"Good for you! After all, he is Julie's only living grandpa."

"No! The only reason he got away was because Abigail showed up, looking haunted and ill. I started feeling sorry for her, and then she let me have it with both barrels."

"God speaks to us in strange ways. He has a plan. Why do you think she showed up at that exact moment— pregnant? Maybe to give you a chance to count your blessings and reconsider getting your revenge. Ransom made a mistake. A long time ago. Yeah, he was too rough on you, but haven't you ever made a mistake? He's an old man now. His wife's sick. The ranch has been in his family for generations. If you hurt him, you hurt Julie."

"I'm through with this conversation."

"Just think about it. Ransom's got plenty of problems without you going after him. Life has a way of making us pay for our sins. If you use Abigail to suit some ambition of yours, you'll regret it."

Connor said goodbye. Leo clicked his mouse, and the computer screen went blank. He sat staring at himself in the gray glare. Then he ran his hands through his hair. After a long time he got up, went to his bar and poured a shot and a half of scotch into a highball glass. Leaning his head back, he bolted it.

Normally, he never drank during the day, and never at his office. The stuff burned his mouth and throat as he sat back down in his leather chair for a long moment and waited for the liquor to ease his pain. When it didn't, he eyed the bottle across the room, yearning for another shot.

No. He'd been down that hellish road. It was always better to face pain, better to stay in control.

Instead, he opened up his top desk drawer and pulled out the file folder with Abigail's name on it that his brother had triumphantly pitched on his desk six weeks ago. Opening it, Leo thumbed through the various documents and photographs.

Several glossy 8 x 10 photos taken with a high-power lens of Abigail riding her golden horse, Coco, fell onto his desk. The DNA report was there, too. He'd told Connor that it was a helluva coincidence her ranch was next to theirs and Shanghai Knight's.

"More than a coincidence," his newly converted, ex-bad-boy brother had retorted with sickening, self-righteous assurance and an easy smile. "It's nothing short of a miracle. God definitely has a plan."

"I don't believe in miracles or plans."

"Someday you will. Maybe sooner than you think."

Leo went to his bookshelf and picked up Julie's picture. She had black hair and black eyes. He'd called her on her last birthday and she'd refused to talk to him. Nancy said that every day she looked more and more like him.

Julie was a teenager now...nearly as old as he'd been when he'd gotten Nancy pregnant. She had a bad attitude about school, said she didn't want to go to college, said she didn't want to do anything but hang out with her friends, who were creeps for the most part. She wanted a tattoo and some piercings. She wore tight clothes and too much makeup. Nancy said it was because she craved attention. Cal said it was because she felt abandoned by her biological father. But what could he do about that when Julie refused to take his calls or see him?

He'd never played a big part in her life, so for all intents and purposes Cal was her father. Now she was nearly grown, and Leo regretted having let his daughter slip away.

Bottom line: how far was he willing to go to prevent that from happening again?

All the damn way, he thought. All the damn way. He'd do whatever the hell it took.

Just one more minute....

The sun was low in the sky, and the shadows of the oaks and pines swept across the gravel road and the lush grasses where Coco grazed nearby.

It had to be close to seven. Abby knew she should get up from the stone bench and go back to the house to wait for Leo. But her heart was thudding because she felt so anxious at the thought of facing him again. She was exhausted, and the balmy warmth soothed her.

Why was it that she could go and go and go—until she stopped? Still, Leo Storm didn't strike her as a patient man, and it would only make things worse if she kept him waiting.

Not that she got up. The soft breeze caressing her cheek was too seductively delicious, and her body felt heavy as she continued to lie flat on her back on the cool stone bench. So instead of doing the intelligent thing, she stayed where she was, procrastinating, enjoying this fleeting moment of peace.

From her first dread-filled, wakeful moment, her day had been long and tense. This was the first second she'd had to herself, if she didn't count the hectic commutes from the ranch to San Antonio, from there to Austin, and then the commute home. The high-speed traffic had been dense and fierce, so there was no comparison to this alone-time lying underneath this wonderful tree.

Trees looked completely different when viewed from such an angle. Lying here took her back to her childhood, and she remembered how much she and Becky had loved climbing trees.

For a moment longer she forgot Leo and lay quietly, staring up at the spreading branches of the immense live oak tree and then beyond at the sparkling sunlight and brilliant blue sky that peeked between the dark leaves. The world was big and the universe even bigger. The problem of her pregnancy and dealing with Leo seemed tiny in comparison until she heard him thrashing clumsily through the trees, calling her name.

"Abby! Abby!"

She shot to her feet at the sound of his deep baritone and brushed a leaf out of her hair. "Over here!"

The intensity of his dark gaze had her trembling long before it slid knowingly to her belly and caused heat to scorch her cheeks. Could he tell that her waist was a little fuller?

She remembered standing on his table. He'd been beneath her as she'd undulated to "Wild Thing" and peeled her red jersey top over her head. When she'd wiggled out of her spandex denim skirt, his avid fascination with her body that night had made her feel feminine and reckless and strangely empowered. Like Pandora's box, once opened, needs had been let out that she was having a hard time containing again. But she had to.

Flecked with gold and rimmed with thick black lashes, his gorgeous eyes had followed her every move. When she was naked, he'd strode to the table, clasped her waist and had pulled her into his arms in such a way that she'd slid down the length of his body.

For a long time he'd simply held her. Then he'd kissed her hair, leaned her back down onto the table very slowly and tongued her body until she'd thought she'd surely turn to flame. She'd wanted wild sex and oblivion from the hurt of years of loneliness. He'd wanted more, and that had scared her.

Don't think about that night. Don't let him that close ever again.

He was tall, six-two at least, and rugged, as well. She knew he did hard, physical work on his ranch, and often when one of her fences had needed mending and she'd driven past while he'd been working on the Little Spur, she'd felt a twinge of envy. It would be nice to have a man around who could do things like that.

His skin was dark, the angular planes of his face thoroughly masculine even when he wore his glasses. He must have gotten home earlier than usual because he'd taken the time to discard his suit and glasses and put on a pair of freshly pressed jeans and a long-sleeved, blue chambray shirt. The soft collar was open at his tanned throat and his sleeves were rolled halfway up his muscular forearms.

Suddenly she wished she'd changed into something more flattering, but she'd been too tired to do anything other than shed her jacket.

She sucked in a breath because just looking at the V of dark hair, and his strong, tanned arms made her feel curiously weak. She had to remind herself that he was serious and dull, not her type at all, that she preferred cowboys and, of course, that he'd taken advantage of her.

Calm down. All you're going to do is talk to him.

"I saw your car, so I knocked," he said. "When you didn't answer, I went around back and found the door open. I yelled, and you didn't answer, so I'm afraid I went on in. When you weren't anywhere…" He stared at her again in that intent way that communicated his fear for her. "Well, never mind now. I've found you. I'm glad you're okay."

His evident concern and even his anger pleased her, which was ridiculous. She didn't want him to care. Most of all, she didn't want to need for him to care. There was nothing to like about him—not now—not after he'd gotten them into this horrible mess.

"Have you eaten?" he asked.

Men and their appetites; they either wanted sex or food.

She shook her head.

"We could drive into town."

"I've driven a lot today. I'm pretty tired. Maybe we could just talk…and then you could go."

"You want to get rid of me as soon as possible?"

"I thought I made it clear that I didn't think we had anything going for us."

"Except good sex…and now the baby."

She didn't deny it, so he pressed his point. "That's a lot to have in common, wouldn't you say?"

"Not nearly enough."

"Okay. Truce. Do you have a beer? It's been a long day."

"You're telling me."

His cell phone went off, and he flipped it open, frowning when he saw who it was. "Sorry. I can't talk now, Connor. Yeah, I'm at her place. No, we haven't gotten to that yet. Hell, no!"

Clearly irritated by whatever his brother had said, he hung up abruptly.

"You told your brother…about us?"

"Yeah. He likes you, so I did. Then he got religious on me. Thinks it's a miracle." He glanced toward her, his eyes both cool and yet disturbingly dark and sensual. "Haven't told anybody else, though. Not yet."

"You're close to your brother?"

"Close enough. We've been through a lot together."

"And you own the Little Spur together, too, right?"

"We both thought it was a good investment. Neither one of us can be here all the time. But we both know a thing or two about ranching, and the physical work after a long day or week at our offices releases a lot of tension."

"I love it out here, too."

"That makes three things we have in common."

Coco walked up and nuzzled him.

"Four. See, your horse likes me."

Abby got up and began to walk toward the house. He

and Coco fell into step beside her. His strides were long and easy, yet his pace matched hers. When she reached her front steps, Abby paused.

"I've got to put Coco in the barn."

"I'll do it," he said.

"But she won't let anybody but me—"

"I've been seducing her with little treats of oats and molasses when I see her along our fence line for quite a while."

"What?"

"Just go inside, and I'll join you in a minute." He headed to the barn with Coco following right behind him.

A few minutes later, when he opened her kitchen door, she nodded for him to come inside. He flashed her a smile and then made a beeline for her refrigerator.

"Give a guy an inch," she began, fighting a smile of her own. "Any problems with Coco?"

"She's a breeze compared to you. Too bad you don't crave oats and molasses…."

He grinned. She grinned back. Then, stooping, he opened the refrigerator and got out two bottles of beer. "Want one?"

"No. Not for the next nine months."

His long glance gently touched on her brow, her nose and last of all her mouth. Heat climbed her neck and scorched her cheeks.

He looked a little embarrassed himself before he turned away to rustle through a drawer. He found an opener and popped the top.

Pulling out a chair, he straddled it. Then, leaning back with a pretense of casualness, he took a long pull from the bottle.

"You certainly know how to make yourself at home," she said.

"Would you prefer to wait on me?"

Turning her back on him, she poured herself a tall glass of water.

"This is probably a bad idea, but I'm prepared to marry you," he said.

She whirled. "Don't do me any damn favors, Storm."

"I was thinking more about giving my child my name."

"Your child? My child, too."

"My point exactly. Our child. People with children do occasionally marry each other."

"For the child's sake?"

"Right. There could be other compensations."

Being a man, he was probably thinking about sex. "We're practically strangers!"

"I disagree. On several counts." His burning black eyes were locked on hers, causing her to blush as dozens of shared intimacies she'd fought to forget flooded her mind. She remembered lying on his bed, her legs parted as he lowered his head to kiss her. Cowboy or not, she hadn't been able to get enough of dull, corporate Leo Storm until long after she'd shuddered against his lips. And not even then. She'd clasped the back of his head and had held him against her for long moments, wanting more, several times. Never had she felt so open, so vulnerable, so completely trusting…or so connected.

Why him? She'd told herself that she couldn't ever let herself feel so vulnerable and trusting again.

She swallowed. "I won't marry you."

"You got a better game plan?"

"Not yet."

"Then that leaves me an open field. But, hey, I'm too hungry to come up with plan B." He set his beer on her kitchen table and went to her refrigerator again. "Why don't I cook us both something for supper?"

Before she could say no, he said, "Or I'm happy to take you out."

He was being entirely too agreeable. "But that would just make everything take longer."

"You mean if I cook, you'll get rid of me sooner?" He was chuckling as he knelt and removed a bag of carrots, two potatoes, mushrooms and two thick, frozen steaks.

Fuming because he didn't appear nearly as upset about all this as she was, she watched in silence as he poked holes in the steak's cellophane wrapper and stuck it in the microwave to defrost.

"You want to watch TV or listen to music while we cook?" he asked as he began clanging pots and pans as if their being together didn't bother him in the least.

"How can you act like everything is perfectly normal, when I'm pregnant and feeling so crazy?"

He put the frying pan down on the unlit stovetop. "I thought maybe we should take our mind off the crisis. And that maybe dinner would help us both to relax a little and get used to each other. That maybe then we could think better."

Relaxing with him was the last thing she wanted to do, but maybe he had a tiny point. "Okay. You're right."

She found her remote and turned on her TV because music sounded romantic and being romantic alone in her house with him scared her. Instantly, she regretted her choice when the news stories were all about crimes of passion. When there was one story after another about men killing their girlfriends, he cursed beneath his breath, picked up the remote and changed the channel to one about the hunting habits of large African cats.

Not that she could focus on pouncing cats tearing throats out of zebras. At least, not with Leo's huge, muscular presence filling her kitchen. His black hair was iridescent as he bent over the stove, and she found herself staring at it and remembering how soft and silky it had felt when she'd slid her fingertips through it. He was so broad-shouldered, she wondered if he'd played football in high school.

Gulping in a quick breath, she got up, grabbed a cutting board, a bag of carrots and a knife, and turned her back on him. Trying to ignore him, she began to cut and chop. But she was very aware of him when he edged closer to her as he washed the lettuce. Only when he went outside and lit her grill could she breathe normally again. But he was back in less than a minute, and so was her tension.

He knew his way around the kitchen; she'd give him that. Dinner preparations certainly went faster when there were two in the kitchen. Twenty minutes later the table was set and the side dishes were simmering. Saying the coals outside were perfect, he salted and peppered their raw steaks and then forked them onto a platter.

"Sun's going down. You want to sit outside and relax with me while I cook our steaks?"

Relax? "What is all this to you? A game?"

"No. But do we have to hate each other forever just because this has happened?"

"Yes. I've taken a vow."

"Have you now?" He headed out the door without

further discussion, letting the screen door bang noisily behind him.

Did he know he was totally stressing her out? Like a little kid with a hankering to bicker, she grabbed a bottle of water and stormed after him.

Not that she said anything when she plopped down in the chair across from his. The instant she sat down, she realized her mistake. The sun was going down in a blaze of scarlet. Stars were popping out in the purple afterglow. The fire and the night air and his closeness made her think romance even though all he was doing was sipping his beer while he watched their steaks. She unscrewed her bottle top and gulped, but an ever-thickening tension caused by the night and his nearness and the intimacies they'd shared was building inside her.

Finally, she blurted, "You know, I was doing just fine before you came along and ruined everything."

"Were you now?" he said easily. "That's why you were in that bar that night dressed in a pickup outfit."

She jumped up off her bench. "I'm single. I'll have you know I have every right to go out with a girlfriend."

"No argument here."

"Nobody tells me what to wear."

"Some outfits do strike a chord in the primitive male psyche, as you probably know."

"I don't have to take this."

For some reason instead of stalking back to the relative safety of her kitchen, she stayed put, her breasts heaving. His dark gaze skimmed the labored breathing of her chest much too appreciatively before he grabbed her wrist and pulled her back down.

"I liked what I saw. Too much. I still do." He paused, his eyes roaming lower than she liked.

"Look at my face, dammit."

He met her glare with an amused look. "Tight denim skirt. Short, too. Tight red jersey top."

"You've got a good memory."

"For things I like. You're a beautiful woman. You wouldn't have worn a getup like that if you hadn't wanted to go home with somebody."

"You took advantage."

"I took what was offered."

"Kel talked me into the bar that night. She said a wild cowboy was the only cure for a broken heart."

"But instead of a wild cowboy, you ended up with me…and a baby."

"Because you pushed."

"Sure I did. I wanted you. I go after what I want."

She'd gone with him because she'd felt lost and vulnerable, and he'd given her the illusory feeling of being protected.

He leaned closer. "And you wanna know something? Despite the way you've treated me lately, I still do. That's why I asked you to marry me. The way I see it, your horse likes me, we wouldn't be so good in bed together if you didn't like me a little, you're pregnant and we've both got places out here. That's a start. Maybe we're not madly in love, but if you tried to get along with me half as hard as you put yourself out to be cantankerous, who knows what might happen?"

"If I tried—"

"Yeah, you! If you did, who knows, maybe things could work out between us."

"You're a calculating guy. I can't believe you're serious about marrying me."

"Believe it."

"What you are suggesting is medieval."

"The Western idea of romantic love is far from universal. Lots of countries believe marriages should be based on more practical reasons. Take the Indians…."

"I am not Indian."

"Their divorce rate is probably lower than ours."

"Something is wrong here. I can feel it. Why are you being so nice when you wouldn't even talk to me this morning?"

"Did anyone ever tell you, you have a suspicious nature?" He shrugged. "Think what you like." He pretended to turn his attention to the fire.

When the steaks were nearly done, he tore off a piece. The gesture was savage, and she wondered if he was as calm and practical about all this as he pretended. "Want to test it?" he asked.

She'd barely nodded before his broad, tanned finger placed a bit of beef on the tip of her tongue.

"Delicious," she murmured, savoring the juicy tidbit.

He let his finger linger against her wet mouth until she turned her head away.

He caught her frightened glance. "What do you say we go inside and eat, woman?"

Four

Leo set his plate on the table, went to the counter and turned off her TV. "I've had my fill of lions. How about some music?"

"No! No music!"

"I seem to remember you got pretty excited over 'Wild Thing.'"

Which had led to a long night of lovemaking.

She remembered tossing him her red jersey top, remembered how he'd inhaled her scent while he'd watched her. The next memory that hit her was how she'd felt when she'd awakened the next morning with his long, lean body sprawled on top of her. She'd been naked, and her body had felt well-used. Her mouth had been bruised from too many kisses and sour with the taste of beer. She'd pushed him away, dressed and run. And she'd never wanted to look back.

But she had, first in her dreams, and then all the time this past week.

"Don't get started on that night!"

"My lips are sealed." He smiled as he sat down across from her at her tiny table. His thigh slid against hers. Funny, how mere denim against black silk could send a frisson of heat up her leg. She jumped back, bumping her knee into the table leg.

"Ouch!"

"Are you okay?" he asked.

Before she could stop him, he knelt to inspect her leg, running his hand beneath the silk and up her calf with unbearable tenderness.

"Good. You didn't even break the skin."

"I'm fine," she muttered through gritted teeth, tugging her pants leg back down.

Smiling broadly, he returned to his seat. "You're mighty jumpy."

Who wouldn't be with him so close? Even seated, he seemed huge. Dangerous. Was he bigger inside her kitchen? Or did the room just seem smaller and more intimate now that darkness pressed its velvet fingertips against the windowpanes and she knew they had the whole night ahead of them.

Slicing off a piece of steak, she tried to concentrate on chewing the tender meat. Impossible with his big muscular body so near…not to mention her memories.

He attempted polite conversation, but when she didn't encourage him, he soon stopped talking. After that, there was only the clatter of forks against china and the beating of her heart. Once or twice they reached for bread at the same time, and their fingers accidentally brushed. Both times she felt a jolt and jumped again while he smiled as if he enjoyed her uneasiness immensely.

The night grew ever darker, and she became ever more intensely aware she was all alone with him in the privacy of her house. A house with bedrooms…and beds. She was as bad as he was. She couldn't get near him without thinking about sex.

Oh, would this interminable meal never end? Would he never finish and get to what they had to discuss and leave?

Marry him? Eat with him every night like this? She would go mad!

He devoured his meal with more relish than she and was finished when she still had half her steak untouched. She wished he'd get up and go out on the porch or something so she could eat in peace, but no, he sat politely watching her toy with a bit of potato until finally she dropped her fork in frustration.

"All done," she whispered raggedly.

"You're sure? You're supposed to be eating for two now, remember?"

As if she needed reminding.

She seized her plate and stood up. "We talk now, and then you go. I've got an early morning just like you do."

"No. First we clear the table and wash and dry your dishes."

"You did say you realized that I'm anxious to get rid of you."

"I suggested dinner. I'm not sticking you with a sink full of dishes. Not when you have an early morning."

"As if you care about that."

"I do. I'm told pregnant ladies tire easily."

He turned from her and put his plate down and

splashed detergent into her sink. She heaved in a breath as he began scraping food into her garbage disposal. There seemed to be no stopping him once he was determined on a path.

"All right…we wash the damn dishes," she muttered, surrendering. "Then we talk and you go."

He was silent at first. Finally he said, "We can talk now. You said no to marriage. Does that mean you prefer money? A large check maybe? Or monthly installments?"

She frowned. "No large check. That sounds so…so cold."

"I agree. I want to assume responsibility for you and the baby. I'd like to know my child…be close to him or her…."

"Under the circumstances, the less you're around, the better."

"Does our baby get a vote?"

She thought better before answering that. Besides, she was too tired to argue.

"In any case," he said, "we'll have to make some legal arrangements—to protect ourselves and the child."

"I can't believe we're having this conversation."

"If we were a normal couple, we'd have fallen in love first."

"But we didn't." The thought made her strangely sad. She didn't believe love made you happy. What it did was make you ache for the impossible.

Studying her face, he lapsed into a thoughtful silence.

He couldn't know that he was making her feel guilty, making her long for things she did not want to long for. Damn the man.

When he dried the last glass, she yanked the dish towel

out of his big tanned hand and threw it on the counter. "Now, you can quit acting so concerned and nice and—"

"Careful." He took a step toward her. "Maybe you shouldn't have reminded me that you go for the bad boys. I might take it as permission to be bad. I've had more experience in that role than you might imagine, and we are very much alone."

"No...." She tried to back away from him, but her hips hit the counter edge.

He followed. Placing a hand on either side of her, he gripped the counter, imprisoning her. "You did go to that bar because you wanted a wild cowboy."

"Stop it."

"Who says only cowboys are wild?"

"Leo, this isn't funny. You were being so nice and so reasonable."

"Nice and reasonable doesn't seem to be working. Maybe you're not the only one here who's been made kinda crazy by what happened that night. I crossed lines, too, lines I've never—" He broke off. "Never mind! I haven't had a date or...woman since that night with you. You want to know why I've been sleeping in town? Well, I'll tell you. Out here I kept wondering about you, wondering if you were over here sleeping alone. Wondering if you'd been out with anyone. Some damn bull rider, maybe, who reminded you of Shanghai. Well, have you? Have you seen other men since me?"

Suddenly he was watching her so intently, she couldn't catch her breath.

"Y-yes... Yes! Many times! That's why I didn't want to see you again."

"I wonder." He was staring down at her mouth, which had suddenly gone dry.

She licked her lips. She wished he'd look away, but he didn't. His gaze burned her mouth. She hoped he couldn't tell she was trembling. She traced her upper lip with her tongue to cool it off. "I think you should go."

"Again we disagree," he said too smoothly, his eyes on her lips.

"You're the enemy."

"Depends on your viewpoint. I'm the father of your child. I want you. Even more now that I know you're pregnant and scared and vulnerable."

"I'm not any of those things!"

"You are, and I think that's a big part of the reason you're so mad at me."

She wasn't about to admit he had a point. She didn't want to feel dependent and needy.

"I hate being pregnant! Why do you get to be so strong and sure of yourself?"

"If you'd let me take care of you, maybe you wouldn't be so scared. Maybe you wouldn't hate being pregnant so much."

"What are you saying?"

"Marry me…at least until after the baby's born."

"But—"

"Look, when the sun came up this morning I didn't want to get married any more than you, but there's our baby to consider now. He'll be legitimate. I think that's important."

"He could be a she."

"Could be, but that's not really the point, is it? People don't think as much of babies who don't have fathers. Don't you want to give our baby the best possible start?"

She hated to agree with him about anything, but she was more old-fashioned than she'd realized. If she didn't marry him, she'd dread telling the baby why she'd never married its father. She'd told Kel, but she felt embarrassed about explaining this mess to the rest of her staff.

"We'll sort it all out as we go along," he said.

He was so close, so tall and dark and strong, and she felt so weary and sad and scared. Would marriage make things better or worse?

Despite her determination to dislike him and blame him, his nearness had an intoxicating effect on her. His clean male scent mingled with something tangy and lemony that she remembered from that night. Her skin had smelled of him afterward. Why couldn't she forget how their bodies had strained together in perfect harmony?

And her dreams... Fragments of half-remembered dreams about him had haunted her when she'd awakened hot and perspiring and clutching her sheets against her breasts in the middle of the night. Did she subconsciously hunger for him even though she fought thinking about him every waking hour?

"This conversation about marriage is ridiculous."

"For a minute there you had the look of a woman seriously considering my offer."

She actually had been. "You've got to go." Desperately, she began pushing at his thick chest.

"Not a good idea," he muttered thickly, crushing her closer.

She knew that if she fought him or screamed, dull,

gentlemanly Leo would let her go. For some reason she stood still in his arms and waited. Maybe to see what he would do next.

When she didn't fight him, something hot and exciting flashed in his dark eyes, but he didn't rush her. His arms stayed around her for another long moment. Then he leaned down, tipped her chin back with a fingertip and kissed her ever so lightly. The instant his mouth grazed hers, a ripple of hot, carnal need trilled from her lips all the way down to her toes.

Not that she was quite past the ability to think and admire his technique. Dull Leo was a superb kisser, her mind noted with cold approval.

His kisses at the bar that night had been the spark that had lit the conflagration that had landed them in this mess.

From that first kiss—a teaser, he'd called it—she'd been his. She remembered his second kiss after he'd told her he was going for broke. Talk about a meltdown.

Her breath came unevenly as she opened her lips. She hadn't realized until his tongue slid against hers how much she'd wanted his mouth and hands on her body again. Was that why she'd dreamed of him and feared him?

Quivering, she threaded her fingertips through the soft black hair that curled over his collar. Then with a little cry, she bunched fistfuls of his shirt, pulled him closer. Breathing hard, he was fully aroused. Holding on tight, she reveled in his passion.

"Where's your bedroom?" he demanded huskily after they'd kissed for a while.

"Right behind us," she answered.

"How convenient."

As his mouth left her lips to explore her neck and

trailed kisses upon her heaving breasts, the enormity of what she was doing washed over her. Weakly, she shoved at his chest. Then she began to push at him and struggle in earnest. But her efforts were puny and half-hearted at best because what she really wanted was Leo naked and wild on top of her. She wanted his knees to spread her legs. She wanted to open herself. She wanted him deep, deep inside her.

"Don't run out on me again," he begged between kisses. One of his big hands slipped down her waist to her knees, and he lifted her into his arms.

When she shook her head and murmured no, he kissed her again and again until she shivered. Then quickly, carrying her, he moved down the dark hall to her bedroom. He set her down on the bed and continued kissing and stroking her. His gaze lit her entire being as he tugged her blue top over her breasts and then over her head. She closed her eyes and lay still as he unhooked her bra and removed it. Very gently he lowered his head, causing her to gasp when he began to lick each rosy brown nipple.

Cupping her breasts, he murmured, "They seem larger." He ran his hand down and rested it on her belly, holding his palm there for a long moment with an attitude of such awe and possession that she began to feel on fire.

His reverence caused a tightness in her throat. Not since Becky had she felt this close to another human being.

Finally, she splayed her fingers against his warm chest. Beneath whorls of dark hair, she felt the violence of his pulsing heart.

He wanted her, but he was a man. He'd said he hadn't

had a woman since he'd been with her. What she couldn't account for was the fierceness of her own urgency.

"Leo…"

Wrapping her arms around him, she leaned her head against his chest with a sigh, reveling in his scent and heat and strength. "I'll regret this. I know it."

She sighed, unable to help herself. Being in his arms felt so right and safe.

What was wrong with spending one more night with him? She was already pregnant, wasn't she? The worst was done…horse out of the barn and all that. She felt strangely light-headed, almost happy knowing she had nothing more to lose and that she could gain such immense pleasure and comfort from letting him make love to her.

"I want you naked," she whispered, knowing she must be mad.

"What?"

"Your turn to strip for me. I stood on that table, re-member."

His gaze burned her.

When he didn't move, she said, "Well, go on."

He gasped as her slim, white hands ripped at his shirt, encouraging him as she yanked it out of his waist-band. When he still did nothing, she undid his belt and unbuttoned his jeans. Last of all, she tugged his zipper down. Never had any sound been more erotic than that rasp of metal as denim parted. When she touched him down there, he groaned loudly.

"Go on," she urged, "take your jeans off."

She removed her hand and stared at his dark body, her heart in her throat as he tore his jeans and shirt and briefs off and tossed them on the floor. There wasn't much moonlight, but there was enough for her to marvel at the heart-stopping perfection of his sculpted, male body. Maybe he was a CEO, but he did more than push pencils. Every inch of his lean body was hard and tough, as lean and tough as any cowboy's.

Dull Leo didn't seem so dull all of a sudden. He danced. He rode. He was great at kissing and great at sex. At least, he was with her. What other hidden talents did he have that could thrill a girl?

She closed her eyes, wanting to know more of him, and yet afraid. So afraid. He was what she'd been running from her whole life.

"Damn you! You'd better not be pretending I'm Shanghai! Not tonight!" he growled fiercely.

Her eyes snapped open, and she saw his cold fury mingle with hurt. "No," she whispered, feeling a strange sympathy. "Only you."

"Good. Tonight I don't want any ghosts in this bed. Just the two of us, understand?"

Swallowing, she nodded. Then she scooted across the bed into a pool of moonlight and kissed him, long and lingeringly on the mouth until they were both breathing so hard, she knew it was way past time for her to take off the rest of her clothes.

He helped her undress. When she was naked, he pulled her beneath the sheets and against his body, which was so blazing hot, she kicked off the covers.

"Why the hell have you been so damn set against me?" he growled.

She arched her body up to meet his. Just to tease him, she began to writhe. "Did anybody ever tell you that you talk too much, Leo Storm?"

Five

Abby awoke to burning heat. Why was she so hot?

When she began to squirm out from under the covers, she realized that she was buried beneath a tumble of sheets and quilts, and her legs and arms were tangled in Leo's. Her first thought was she'd better get out of bed and call Kel to warn her she'd be late getting into the office again. But Leo's warmth lulled her.

Who cared about the office anyway? Kel could handle anything, and from what Abby had seen of Miriam, she imagined Miriam could, too. Unlike the first morning after they'd made love, Abby did not disentangle herself and run. Instead she lay there, savoring the memories of his touches and intimacies of the night before.

Last night, dull Leo had definitely been anything but. Again and again she'd driven him over the edge until he'd clasped her, rasping for every breath, groaning her name as he'd shuddered in her arms.

He'd been so reasonable and nice all evening, cooking supper, washing dishes, putting up with her mood. Had he been intent on this happening all along?

He'd made love to her with such passionate, primal determination—as if he'd been staking his claim and making her his. It had all been very primitive and wild, and just thinking about it made her shiver and feel reluctant to leave the bed.

She stretched, reliving each and every one of the torrid memories. No man had ever wanted her with such intense urgency, and she had certainly responded in kind.

A black lock fell over his dark brow. She marveled that the sharp angles of his virile features could seem so much softer this morning. He'd been so driven and relentless last night.

Despite his dark, unshaven chin, he looked as innocent as a small child. At the same time he looked like a man who'd gotten exactly what he'd wanted.

She was still marveling at his look of contentment when his black eyes lazily opened and met hers, claiming her.

His arm came around her possessively, and he grinned, showing off his perfect white teeth. "Good. You're still here."

"It's my bed. My house," she said. "Where would I go?"

"So—are you going to marry me?"

"There are a million logical reasons why that's a very bad idea."

"You're pregnant. If we're unhappy, we'll get a divorce. Big deal."

"Divorce *is* a big deal."

Her parents had divorced. She still wasn't over it. She'd always dreamed of a romantic start at marriage, of making it work. "I can't just marry—casually."

When she started to ease away from him, he bolted upright, and the tension became palpable between them. He looked fiercely masculine.

"Stay here a minute," he whispered.

She sucked in a breath and swallowed.

"Please. I need to tell you some things."

"Okay."

"I got a girl pregnant when I was a kid. I won't go into the whole story now, but I couldn't marry her. For one thing, she wouldn't marry me. Hell, maybe it was for the best. That's what I try to tell myself. But, I hardly know my daughter, Julie, and I regret that more every day. So, your pregnancy isn't just about me and you, you know."

The pain in his voice touched her deeply.

"I'm older, settled in a career. I have plenty of money. I can afford a wife and child. I would try very hard to make our relationship work."

But he didn't love her, and she didn't love him. Maybe that was a good thing. Maybe when they divorced, she wouldn't suffer so much. If they married, at least their child would never have to be ashamed of the circumstances surrounding its birth.

She mulled over his proposal for a long time. Finally, she met his gaze again. "I know this is crazy. I know it won't work. I'll regret it. But for the baby…yes."

"Hey," he said gently. "How can you still be so damn negative after last night?"

Before she could tell him that sex, even great sex,

wasn't really all that important in marriage, he rolled onto his back and pulled her down on top of him.

"So, we're getting married," he said as if that was going to take some getting used to. "How about that?" His gaze was tender as he kissed her lightly on the brow.

When she didn't budge—fool that she was, was she actually hoping for more?—he said, "I'd better brush my teeth and shower so we can get to our offices."

He went into her bathroom, and her shower ran for quite a while. Later, when he appeared in her kitchen, his wet black hair gleamed, and his breath smelled like peppermint.

Dull Leo Storm was nothing if not fastidious.

"How about a cup of coffee, *dear?*" she quipped.

"*Dear?* I like the sound of that. Coffee sounds good, too, but I can get that anywhere. I'd rather have a kiss…from my bride to be."

"Hmm." Slowly she went into his arms and nestled close as if she belonged there.

He grinned. "I've just got time for one kiss, so I'd better go for broke. Don't want you changing your mind as soon as I drive off."

"Going for broke… That's what you said the night you got me pregnant."

He smiled as she lifted her lips to his. One taste, and they were both starving again. She really did think maybe she ought to promote Kel and give her more executive responsibilities.

"I've got an early meeting," he muttered several kisses later when things had really begun to heat up. "Buy a white dress and veil and decide who you want to be at our wedding. I'll handle the rest of the arrangements and call you back about the date. Let's get married as fast as possible—say in a week or ten days."

"A week? Weddings take a lot of time."

"Trust me. A week!" His quick male smile was both superior and all-knowing.

Men. Women could spend a year orchestrating a wedding. Being a CEO, he'd probably dictate his guest list, turn the arrangements over to the hard-hearted Miriam and think nothing more about it.

Ten minutes later when he loped out to his truck, Abby followed him, still feeling bemused. He kissed her again on the bottom step. Then she stayed there, licking her mouth, tasting him as she watched until his truck disappeared in clouds of red dust.

Her bruised lips were still warm from his kisses. She was wondering if he'd come back tonight and make love to her again. How could she want that? How she could feel almost happy about this, when so much could go wrong?

Was it because he was so good in bed? Yes, that had to be it. After last night, she was still in a brain fog. When she came to her senses, would she even like him?

Doomed. Abby felt trapped and alone as she stood beside Leo one week later before the carved altar of Mission San José in front of a hundred wedding guests, pledging herself in marriage.

If only her father had showed up, just this once. She thought about Becky and her long-dead mother and the perfect marriage and family she'd dreamed about having someday.

She missed the family she'd lost so much, missed

her father. Here she was, alone, marrying a man she barely knew.

"You may kiss the bride," the preacher said, his deep, sonorous voice ringing inside the thick stone walls of the ancient mission chapel.

As Leo's warm lips touched hers, Abby began to shake with the realization she was now married to this darkly handsome stranger. Was it only a week ago that he'd proposed and she'd marveled that he'd thought he could arrange everything so quickly?

Except for the night he'd dropped by to slide a three-carat engagement ring onto her finger, she'd hardly seen him. Miriam, however, had called her constantly to confirm various details. If Miriam was surprised by this sudden turn of events, she'd given no indication. She'd been deferential, respectful and, above all, exceedingly capable and efficient.

All Abby had had to do was buy a dress, invite her father, her friends and her staff…and show up. Not that her father had made the effort to do even that. He'd promised he'd be here to give her away, but an hour before the wedding, he'd called her on her cell with an excuse, wishing her the best wedding day ever but saying that his flight out of Colombia—where he was interviewing terrorists in the jungle—had been cancelled. As always, the adrenaline high he got from hanging out with a dangerous terrorist was a bigger lure than anything having to do with her, so Leo's brother, Connor, had given her away.

Even as Leo's warm lips lingered over hers, her father's absence tugged at her heart.

"It's okay," Leo whispered, releasing her. "He'll make it next time."

How had he known what she was thinking? That seemed sweet until a thought occurred to her and new fears filled her eyes. Was he already thinking of their imminent divorce and her future marriage to another man?

"Next time?" she asked in a tremulous tone.

Sensing her doubt, he squeezed her hand. "When the baby's born."

Still gripping her hand, Leo turned to face the congregation with his new bride. For an instant she was aware of Leo staring at his brother. In a sea of happy faces, Connor was the only man who looked grim. Leo smiled, so she forced a smile, too. When everyone stood, Connor was the last to rise, and he didn't join in the joyous applause for the couple. Was Connor, who knew the situation, as dubious about their union's ultimate success as she?

Leo's guest list had turned out en masse. Not counting his glum-looking brother, most of the guests worked for the Golden Spurs. She'd met many of them when she'd gone down to the Golden Spurs to wait for Shanghai to bring Mia back from Mexico after he'd rescued her.

Joanne Kemble, the late Caesar Kemble's widow and the mother of Mia and Lizzy Kemble, was the first to rush up to them and congratulate Leo.

"My, you're certainly a dark horse," she said a little too brightly. "You didn't even bring a date to the ranch for our Memorial Day family reunion. And a week later you call me and tell me you're getting married? Who is this woman who could make you change course with the speed of light?"

Leo's face darkened. "It happened suddenly."

"You're an ambitious man. You never make a move without thinking about it from every angle. You hardly seem the type to rush into marriage."

"It's called falling in love," Leo said, shooting Abby a tender glance. "Cupid's arrow is but one of the many reasons why it is impossible to predict the behavior of any human being."

"Well, someday I hope to learn the whole story." Joanne's all-knowing, speculative gaze zeroed in on Abby and stayed there, making her feel the woman saw too much. "Your bridegroom called every guest and invited each of us personally. He bragged and bragged about you. He said you were beautiful and smart. He sounded so in love. It was really...quite sweet. I had to change some vacation plans, but I wouldn't have missed this. Not for the world! Leo married. Who would have thought?" She paused. "I can't tell you what an asset he is to the Golden Spurs. And you will be, too, I'm sure."

Only she didn't sound sure.

"Still, this will certainly take some getting used to. I'm afraid we keep him hopping with all our crises. But he's so cool and collected. So logical. So ambitious—globally—for the ranch. He has a way of solving problems with the least emotional energy and the greatest efficiency, which is great, since we Kembles seem to have a flair for drama." She paused, her eyes growing even more intense. "How's your father?"

At the sudden unfortunate change of topic, Abby started guiltily. "He couldn't come."

"And I was so looking forward to seeing him." Joanne looked away.

"You know him?"

Joanne blushed. "Y-yes. Not all that well—I mean, personally—but he is a famous man…at least in some circles."

Abby felt she was missing something. She had never considered her father famous even though he was a multipublished, award-winning, nonfiction writer. "He's in Colombia, working. His plane was cancelled at the last minute. He really wanted to be here."

"I'm sure. Your father is so dedicated." Joanne's forceful, veined hands were cool and yet perspiring as they clung to Abby's. "I admire his work so much."

"Many people do."

"I wish…." The older woman blushed again and then frowned. "Never mind. Just tell him that I—I…that Joanne Kemble said hello."

"I will."

Joanne's gaze held hers a moment longer. There was depth and hope and an inexplicable tension in her gaze, but before Abby had time to dwell on this, a woman named Mona called to her, and Joanne turned and ran eagerly, as if welcoming the chance to escape a conversation that had felt increasingly awkward to them both.

What had that been about?

For a long moment, Abby felt confused and a little lost even though she was surrounded by people and Leo stood at her side with his hand on her elbow.

Joanne seemed to know her father very well indeed, and she'd taken much too great an interest in Abby for comfort. She would have to ask her father about Joanne Kemble someday.

Mia and Shanghai Knight and their dark-haired little girl, Vanilla, were the next to come up. Shanghai held her hand too tightly and kissed her a little more passionately than was proper for a former boyfriend. Was he relieved to have her safely married?

"You're a lucky man, Storm," he said gruffly, shaking his hand after releasing Abby. "You'd better take good care of her. You know you can't work as hard with a new bride."

Leo nodded, rather fiercely she thought.

"Hey, maybe you two could buy me out of the Buckaroo Ranch since your ranches both touch mine on different corners. I don't get up there much since I married Mia."

Leo nodded again. He didn't look like he was enjoying Shanghai kissing Abby or talking to them much. Then Vanilla raced away. Shanghai laughed and, catching Leo's eye, said, "Well, that's my cue. I'd better go," and chased after her. Mia laughed and followed after them at a more leisurely pace.

Funny, Abby didn't feel the least bit jealous of Mia anymore.

"Maybe we *should* buy him out of the Buckaroo," Leo said.

Shanghai's brother, Cole Knight, strode up with his wife, Lizzy, Mia's sister.

Kel, who was next in line, hugged Abby and quietly told her that if she was going to keep the baby, marriage to a guy as cool as Leo was definitely the best way to go.

"He's not the least bit dull. And he holds his own pretty well with all these hunky Golden Spurs cowboys. He's handsome and suave. And he's got to be smart. Still, I can't believe a straight guy could pull this off," Kel said.

"This?"

"You. This wedding. I mean, an historical mission—

the queen of missions, no less—what a great venue for a wedding! So memorable and romantic. And he did it in a week! Cool! Everything's simply gorgeous. Even the weather cooperated." She began to rave about the band and caterer.

Kel knew a thing or two about event planning since everybody who worked at In the Pink! had to constantly arrange photo shoots and coordinate media events, too often with very little notice.

"It's a little too perfect, and it was a little too easy for him, if you ask me," Abby said moodily.

"You'd prefer to be marrying a doltish, wild cowboy with no social aptitude?"

"Let's not go there. Just don't give him too much credit. His secretary probably did everything."

Kel, who thought secretaries ran the world, nodded. "Well, who hired her? Who keeps her happily working? You'd better watch out. Now that he's got a smart wife to go along with his super-brilliant secretary, he'll be invincible."

When the next person in line nudged Kel, she said, "I think I'll go introduce myself to his hunky brother. What was his name?"

"Connor. Over there…."

She nodded toward Connor, who was standing beneath a live oak tree with a glass of champagne in his hand. Why did he keep studying his brother so deliberately?

Connor was an investigator, she told herself. He was probably suspicious by nature. Maybe he thought she'd trapped Leo and felt protective of his older brother.

There were champagne toasts and dancing. Not that Abby drank anything other than sparkling water. Leo held her close when they danced, too close, and she was reminded that dancing close was what had led to that first going-for-broke kiss in the bar that had made her decide to go home with him.

She and Leo cut the cake and fed each other, licking cake and icing off each other's lips. When she passed on the white wedding cake and ate only the groom's chocolate cake, he made her confess that she was something of a chocoholic.

On the surface the reception was gay and happy, but Abby couldn't ignore Connor's unsmiling face every time his glance fell upon his brother or her. Nor could she forget her own doubts or Joanne's awkward comments. This was a marriage of convenience—not a real marriage. And, therefore, not a happy occasion.

Still, why dwell on those things? Maybe she would have stopped worrying if she hadn't overheard a snippet of the brothers' hushed conversation when they thought she was distracted by Miriam.

"So, have you told her?" Connor demanded.

"Butt out!" Leo replied.

"If you don't, and someone else… If she learns what you did that night from someone else, there will be hell to pay."

"You heard me," Leo said.

Abby must have made some sound, because they turned, and, when Connor met her gaze, he broke off in mid-sentence. Flushing darkly, both men rushed up to her.

You married a stranger.

She'd been a fool to go through with this, she thought miserably even as Leo took her hand reassuringly and tucked her possessively against his tall body.

"Told me what?" she asked.

"Sorry?" Leo said, frowning as if in confusion.

"I couldn't help overhearing…."

"We were talking about business. Dull stuff. I hire Connor from time to time."

"What do you need a private investigator for?"

Joanne, who'd been standing nearby chatting to Mona, was suddenly beside them again. "Oh, that's Lizzy's fault," she said, staring at Abby in that way that made her so uncomfortable. "I don't know how much you know about our family, but my late husband had two daughters by another woman, who was rather famous. Electra Scott. Have you heard of her?" A shrill edge had crept into her voice.

Leo's mouth thinned. The color drained from his face. Everyone around them fell silent and looked uneasy, too. Not that Joanne backed off. She seemed hellbent on making some point.

"Oh, yes," Abby finally said. "I believe I have. Electra Scott. Didn't she die recently? In some jungle?"

"Yes." Joanne's eyes were as coldly blue as ice shards.

"And she took wonderful pictures of children and animals and wildlife?"

"Among other things," Joanne said.

"I think maybe my father may have collaborated on a book with her," Abby said.

"Did he? Well, that wouldn't surprise me. They were both well-known."

Leo was frowning and shifting his weight from one foot to the other, but again Joanne ignored him.

"Electra was my best friend in college. She was incredibly adventurous and very…independent. Lots of fun back then. She wasn't made for marriage. She always said, she'd never settle down. That life had too many possibilities. 'Why should I only live one little life, in one country, with one man?' she used to say.

"I brought her to the ranch, and Caesar fell madly in love with her the second he set eyes on her. I was in love with his older brother, Jack, who died, back then."

"I'm sorry."

"Thank you." An ugly shadow passed across Joanne's face. "But it was a very long time ago. I'd grown up knowing the Kembles, so after Jack died and Electra went away, Caesar and I eventually married. Not long after his death, I came into possession of Electra's journal and discovered that Electra had secret twin daughters by Caesar. Eventually Lizzy insisted we ask Leo to find them, and he hired Connor." She looked from Abby to Connor, her eyes seeming to ask much more than her question. "So, how's that coming?"

Leo's hand tightened ever so slightly on Abby's. When she glanced at him, he smiled and deliberately relaxed his fingers.

"I've made some real progress, but lately I've hit a few snags," Connor said, his eyes glued to his brother like an actor waiting for a cue. "Hopefully we'll have some good news for you before long."

Leo heaved in a breath and managed a thin smile. Not that his eyes warmed.

"How old would his daughters be now?" Abby asked, curious about these secret sisters.

"Twenty-six…nearly twenty-seven."

"Like me." Abby looked at Connor. "And these missing twins…they have no idea that they're Kembles?"

Joanne froze. "No. I am quite sure they don't. And it may come as quite a shock when they find out." Then, without another word, she turned and walked away.

Lifting his glass of champagne, Connor gulped it dry. "It's late. I'd better go." He turned to leave without so much as a glance toward his brother.

His abrupt departure, as well as Joanne's, struck Abby as odd.

"Is your brother happy about our marriage?" Abby asked when she was alone with Leo.

"Of course. What makes you ask?"

"I don't know him, but he seems…worried. And Joanne… I don't think she likes me."

"You're wrong about Joanne. As for Connor, he's always been moody. I should know. I raised him. I'm sure it has to do with work. He takes his work very seriously."

Leo's mouth was tight, and he seemed edgily defensive. Abby sensed he probably knew more than he was willing to admit. "Like you say, you know him. I don't. Whatever his misgivings, at least Connor showed up. Unlike my—"

"Your father would have been here if he could have been."

"It's easy for you to believe that. But then you don't know him like I do, do you?"

"Right." As if stung, he shut up.

She was remembering all the school performances her father had missed. He hadn't come to even one, not even those in which she'd starred. She thought about the Christmas card in her drawer that had arrived two weeks late.

This wasn't a real marriage. What did it matter if Joanne acted strange or Connor disapproved or her father wasn't here? Leo, who looked as tight and strained as she felt, took her hand and brought it to his lips. "I'm sorry," he said, squeezing her fingers.

She looked away just as an older man, who introduced himself to her as B. B. Kemble, came up and began to rant about the high winds and drought in South Texas. Leo fell into this discussion with relish, probably because he was anxious to forget her and about their tense conversation. Soon he was smiling again, and she was sure he'd forgotten her entirely. So, feeling lost and forgotten, she let go of his hand and wandered away.

All too soon the reception was over and Leo and she were holding hands again. Bending low, they ran through their guests, who blew environmentally correct bubbles over their heads as they made a dash for Leo's waiting stretch limousine, which whisked them toward the center of the city.

Leo hadn't attempted conversation since they'd discussed Connor and her father. When the driver didn't take the downtown exit that would have taken them to Leo's loft apartment, Abby tugged at Leo's sleeve.

"Airport. Weekend honeymoon," Leo said brusquely. "Sorry I can't get away for longer. Didn't Miriam tell you to pack a bag?"

"She said, 'Be prepared for warm weather. Two nights. And be sure to bring a bathing suit.' I thought she meant you had a pool in your building."

"I do. But Miriam was wrong about the bathing suit. Where we're going, it's so private, we can swim naked. I hope you'll want to."

The sudden heat in his eyes made her breath catch. "Where are we going?"

"It's a surprise."

She couldn't stop looking at her lean-muscled husband. With his black hair and tanned skin, he was devastatingly, moody-broody handsome. Fierce looking, too.

Her heart sped up. Boy or girl, their baby would be beautiful if it looked anything like him.

Leo held out his hand. When she took it, he pulled her closer. Her head fell against his shoulder, and the rasp of his warm breath in her hair made her scalp tingle.

That first night they'd made love, he'd held her curled against him like this for hours. She'd fallen asleep as if drugged from his lovemaking, never wanting to leave his arms—only to wake the next morning to profound guilt at her wanton behavior.

They'd both been forced into this marriage. They barely knew each other. What chance did their marriage have?

Six

When Abby and Leo got off the Golden Spurs jet, warm, humid, salt-laden air blew her hair back from her face. The inky sky swam with stars, and she could hear the surf pounding noisily.

The airport was a strip of asphalt laid on top of sand. Palm fronds clattered noisily beside a lone hangar at the end of the strip.

"Where are we?" she cried as he hurried her through blowing grit toward a strange-looking beach buggy.

"A private barrier island off the Texas coast. It's owned by a Texas rancher and oilman who owes me a favor or two. He offered to let me use his beach house for our honeymoon. His house is about a mile down the beach."

Even if the beach house hadn't been vast, yet cozy, she would have been glad to get inside and out of the wind. Nestled behind towering sand dunes and surrounded by dense vegetation, which included lots more noisy palms, the mansion had the ambience of a Caribbean plantation house. Big open rooms made for stunning interiors with soaring beamed ceilings and furnishing in beiges and browns with the occasional bright plump cushion and potted plant.

Leo ended his tour of the immaculate house in the master bedroom. Beside a massive, textile-draped, four-poster bed, a magnum of champagne and a bottle of sparkling water stood side by side chilling in a silver ice bucket.

As Leo deftly opened the champagne and poured himself a glass, she wondered who kept the mansion in such pristine shape and where Leo's pilot would sleep tonight. Not that she asked.

Leo opened the water and poured a glass for her. When he handed her hers, he tipped his glass toward hers, and she did the same. Crystal clinked.

He didn't make a toast out loud, however, she eyed the bed and made one silently. *To luck. To miracles. To happiness…together…forever.* She knew she was naive to even entertain such hopes.

"You look scared," he said. "At times like this, try to remember that Coco likes me."

"That's definitely a big point in your favor." Another point was the fact that he'd hired an excellent groom to take care of Coco while she was pregnant.

"I'll take all the points I can get," Leo said.

He smiled at her as she lifted her glass. When she gulped deeply, his smile broadened. He was about to lift his to his lips, when his cell rang.

He frowned when he saw who it was and excused

himself. "I've got to take this. Why don't you get ready for bed?"

The word *bed* was still hanging heavily in the air as he let himself out onto the balcony so he could speak privately.

Why was he being so secretive? Was this a business call or personal? She remembered Connor's grim attitude. What was going on?

Have you told her?

What if Connor had been referring to her? Leo had definitely seemed more strained since she'd asked him about their conversation.

Well, the empty bedroom wouldn't give her any answers. It was late. She decided to take Leo's advice and get ready for bed.

A wedding dress wasn't the only purchase she'd made when she'd gone shopping. She'd bought several sheer nightgowns, as well.

Hesitating for a moment, she went to her suitcase and removed her toiletries and the filmiest of all her new nightgowns, which was a transparent beige.

In the marble bathroom, she undressed and showered. She opened her legs and lathered herself. For long moments she let the warm water run down her neck and her breasts to her belly and thighs. Even after all the bubbles were gone, she stood under the water thinking about the two nights she'd spent with Leo.

He was so sexy. He could do anything, everything to a woman. She'd thought a corporate type like him would be unimaginative in bed, but he had no inhibitions. And he'd made her forget hers. Now that they were married, she wondered if he'd be willing to fulfill her wildest fantasies.

The tensions of the wedding and the reception drained away, and an all-consuming fiery hunger ate at her. He hadn't slept with her since she'd agreed to marry him. She wanted him—again. Just thinking about it made her heart beat faster and faster.

She turned off the water, stepped out of the shower and ripped a towel off a bar. Drying herself and her hair, she pulled the nightgown over her head. Last of all, she brushed her teeth so that she'd taste of peppermint, since peppermint seemed to be Leo's favorite flavor.

Racing into the bedroom, she turned out the lights, got into bed and waited for him to return. When thirty minutes passed and he still hadn't come, she got up and opened the doors to the balcony.

There was nothing out there but the screaming palms, the roar of the surf and the blowing sand. She slammed the doors and leaned against them. Where was Leo? Why hadn't he come to bed? Didn't he want her?

Had he had his fill of her already? Did he feel trapped and therefore uninterested? Some part of her wasn't quite ready to believe that. And yet…how well did she really know him?

Without bothering to search for her robe, Abby left the bedroom in search of Leo. When she heard his deep baritone issuing commands as decisively as a general, she ran down the hall. Pushing open the last door, she found him seated at a huge desk in the study, holding two phones, one against each ear.

She paused in the middle of the door so that the hall light came from behind her.

His gaze met hers and then ran the length of her backlit body before returning to her face. Something dark and powerful made his eyes flame. She read male appreciation and maybe more. Whatever his emotion, he turned it off with an abruptness that chilled her. Closing his eyes and then opening them, he regarded her levelly.

"Just a second," he said in a hard voice to whoever was on the phones.

Frowning, he shook his head at her. "Sorry. There's a grass fire at the Golden Spurs. It's huge, and it's my fault because I authorized a controlled burn yesterday. The fire jumped a road and got away from our men. The grass is dry and the wind is horrible. I should have gone down there myself to see to it. But I didn't."

Because he'd married her.

Not that he seemed to blame her.

"I have to deal with it now. Go to bed. I'll sleep in here near the phones. No need for us both to be up all night."

"I don't mind the phone ringing, if only you'll come to bed."

"We'll see," he said. "Maybe later."

"It's our honeymoon."

"I know." A muscle in his cheek jumped, but he lowered his head, his complete attention on his callers again.

Feeling rejected and desolate, Abby lay awake most of the night. She tossed this way and that, her emotions tearing at her. When she did sleep, she had weird dreams. Connor kept appearing in them like a dark spirit with his constant refrain.

Have you told her?

Every time she woke up, she felt like a fool for wanting Leo so much and even more of a fool for feeling so hurt because he preferred the study to being with her. Three weeks ago she hadn't ever wanted to see him again, and now she was pining after him like a lovesick idiot—just because she was a romantic when it came to marriage.

Around five o'clock, she got up and tiptoed down the hall to check on him. She found Leo, still dressed in his tux, asleep in the big leather chair in the brilliantly lit study. He looked so tired, she didn't want to wake him and urge him to come to bed. All she did was turn off the lights and cover him with a soft throw. Then she returned to the master bedroom and lay down alone. Finally, she fell into a dreamless sleep.

An hour or so later he walked into the bedroom and checked on her. She heard him, but false pride made her pretend to be asleep.

He neither spoke nor touched her. He simply stood there watching her "sleep" as she'd watched him. He walked back to his study, and her heart ached as she listened to his retreating footsteps falling ever softer as he moved back down the length of the hall.

Once more she drifted to sleep, awakening a few hours later to the smell of coffee. She combed her hair, put on her makeup and dressed in white shorts, a T-shirt and sandals. Hoping the fires were out and his mood improved, she scampered down the hall and found him in the kitchen talking on his cell again. Only this time, when he saw her, he ended the conversation abruptly.

"Sleep well?" he asked, his face grave.

She nodded, not wanting to admit how much she'd longed for him.

"And you?" She tried to sound casual.

"Not the best night, but I've had worse." His weary

smile failed to reach his eyes. "I'll make you some breakfast."

"What about the fire?"

"Not good. I'm afraid I have to go down there as soon as possible. I'll fly you to San Antonio. Then I have to go to the Golden Spurs. Ten thousand acres have burned. We've lost several structures. The fire seems to be getting worse. We need to cut or hose down the grass on either side of more ranch roads to make firebreaks and move cattle."

"Wouldn't you get there faster…if I went with you?"

"Yes, but I don't expect…" His black eyes narrowed. "I mean the Golden Spurs is my concern. Not yours."

His expression changed, and she wondered what he was thinking

"What?" she said.

"Nothing," he muttered grouchily.

"I'm going with you then. It's my concern now, too. I'm your wife."

"Suit yourself." His face remained guarded and impossible to read, but he nodded.

After a long moment, he said, "Look, I'm sorry I'm such bad company. I just got word that Black Hawk and Chinook helicopters capable of pouring hundreds of gallons of water in one sweep can't join our firefighters until the winds decrease. By the way, my pilot's standing by."

"I can be ready in five minutes."

"No, first we eat. I'm pretty tired after last night, but it wasn't anything compared to what's in store for us."

Like before at her house, he was at ease in a kitchen. Within minutes they were seated at the table in front of freshly squeezed orange juice, eggs, toast and bacon. Even though a maid would probably be flown in to tidy the place, he cleaned the kitchen perfectly. Then they packed, and he carried her bags to the dune buggy.

"Sorry that we didn't have much of a honeymoon," he said once they were airborne and she was glancing wistfully down at the house on the island and the strip of long white beach in front of it.

Not that he seemed sorry. His face was tense and drawn. He was completely preoccupied by his worries about the fire. Still, every few minutes she caught him watching her, almost in the same way that Connor had watched him during their reception, as if he really were worried about something concerning her, too.

Connor's question kept repeating itself in her mind. *Have you told her?*

Was she being self-centered to think he'd been talking about her?

Fifty miles out from the ranch headquarters of the Golden Spurs giant plumes of smoke billowed higher than a mountain against a hellish, purple-orange sky. When they got closer she could see cowboys on horseback were moving cattle. Leo went to the cockpit and ordered the pilot to fly low all over the ranch. He took pictures and made notes while talking constantly to Kinky Moore, the ranch's foreman, on his cell phone.

When they finally landed behind the tall, red-roofed Big House and its outbuildings, the air was heavy with the acrid smell of smoke. A white sun burned a hole through the slate-gray sky. Winds whipped the mesquite and palm trees on every side of her. Kinky ran up to them and told Leo that because of the wind direction, the house wasn't threatened.

"We've got a hunting lodge to hose down and cattle to move just south of Black Oaks. Mia, Cole and Shanghai are down there now trying to save the old Knight homestead at Black Oaks."

Leo studied the black sky and then turned to her. "I shouldn't have brought you down here. The fire's bigger and closer to the house than I realized."

"There was no time to do anything else. I'll be fine."

"Stay inside until I come back. Keep your cell phone charged and handy." He turned to go.

"I want to go with you."

"No!"

She would have argued, but Leo's expression was harsh and unyielding. And the situation was too chaotic. Fire trucks and bulldozers were everywhere. Adrenaline charged the air. Exhausted-looking firemen streaked across the lawn in dirty orange overalls, shouting orders over cell phones and bickering with sweat-streaked, soot-faced cowboys about how best to fight the fire.

When the cowboys saw Leo, they shouted and waved to him, and before she knew it, he'd left her to join the quarrel between the cowboys and the firemen.

The firemen wanted to start some controlled burns, but the cowboys yelled that if the wind changed, they'd lose valuable livestock and maybe the Big House. Leo battled long and hard, speaking in a firm, rational voice, but the firemen refused to listen and soon sped away in their fire trucks to start more burns.

A second later Leo was on his phone again. "Shanghai! The firemen are going to set pasture seven on fire! We've got hunting lodges down there, and if the wind changes—"

Then Leo was running, shouting to Kinky. As the two men got in Kinky's big black SUV, Abby ran up to them and grabbed Leo's door handle.

"Leo… Take care."

His hair was unkempt, his countenance hard and carved with exhaustion and worry. She wanted him to get out of the SUV and pull her into his arms and crush her close, to press his mouth to hers, to say something, anything, before he left, but his dark face remained frozen even as his black eyes seared her.

Kinky twisted the key in the ignition, and the big vehicle roared to life.

"Leo… Don't leave me."

He clenched his jaw and nodded to Kinky to go.

Her last glimpse of him etched itself into her mind. Broad shoulders, steel-like jaw, anxiety emanating from him, virile sexiness.

What if he never came back?

Her heart felt hollow. A fist squeezed her throat closed.

Except for two nights of sex, she barely knew this man. How could she feel this intensely about him when, obviously, he didn't return her feelings?

Her shoulders sagged hopelessly as she backed away from the SUV. She didn't matter. She never mattered. He was leaving her, just like Becky had…just like her parents had. Everybody always left her.

Speechless, motionless, she watched Kinky back the big vehicle out of its space and then edge out onto the road. A minute later the SUV vanished in the thickening smoke.

She notched her chin up. Nothing had changed. She'd been alone for years and years. She had to get a grip. She couldn't let illusions about marriage and what it should mean and her growing attraction for this man make her hope for something impossible.

When she went into the house and descended the stairs to the basement, she found Sy'rai Moore, whom she'd met at her reception, downstairs in the kitchen, cooking and washing dishes along with Lizzy and Joanne. Off in one corner, Vanilla was on the floor building a high wall out of a set of blocks. From time to time, Joanne would fold her dish towel, kneel and add a block to the towering structure, which Vanilla would knock down and then rebuild.

Cowboys and firemen were down at the house between shifts. The men were smiling and laughing, fighting valiantly to pretend they were cheerful and brave as they sat at tables in small dining rooms off the kitchen, eating beans, charred venison, roasted nilgai antelope, gravy and mashed potatoes.

Sy'rai told her they'd hurried home as soon as they found out about the fire and repeated that Mia, Shanghai and Cole were struggling to save the Knight's ancient homestead.

Not wanting to dwell on her fears for Leo, Abby grabbed an apron. "What can I do?"

"Same thing we're doing," Joanne said. "We've got a lot of tired, hungry men."

By six o'clock the smoke was so thick in the basement that Abby's throat burned and her eyes and nose ran constantly. News reached them that things were bad near Black Oaks. Panicking, she tried to call Leo to find out what was going on over there, but he never answered.

The television anchormen gloomily reported that more than thirty thousand acres were on fire and that a wind shift was expected. "There have been two fatalities on the Golden Spurs Ranch over near Black Oaks, but the names of the individuals are being withheld until their families can be notified."

Panic cut through Abby. With her heart pounding in her throat, Abby dialed Leo again. Still no answer. What if…?

She clutched the phone against her chest as aerial shots showed one hunting lodge exploding in flames. Just as the camera panned to the homestead at Black Oaks, reduced to a pile of burning, red-hot rubble, Kinky stalked into the kitchen.

Sy'rai ran to him and threw her arms around him. His face and clothes were black with soot; his voice hoarse. His dark eyes held no emotion.

"Leo…is Leo with you?" Abby whispered.

He shook his head. Then his weary eyes passed over her. "We're evacuating the headquarters. Everybody get your stuff and be ready to get the hell out of here! We've got thirty minutes max!"

"But have you seen Leo?"

"What about Cole…and Mia and Shanghai?" Lizzy asked.

Without looking at Lizzy, Kinky shook his head. "Last I saw of them, they were in the thick of it over there at Black Oaks. You saw the pictures on TV. You know as much as I do."

"But you drove him over there," Abby cried.

"Drove him into hell. That's what I did."

Kinky stomped back up the stairs and began yelling orders. Soon cowboys were lifting priceless antiques and paintings and carrying them out of the house to load into the beds of their pickups.

Frantic, Abby punched in Leo's number again. When he still didn't answer, she ran outside where Lizzy and Sy'rai had begun hosing down the house and grounds and nearby trees with garden hoses.

Sy'rai was hooking more hoses together to make them long enough for her to haul one up the stairs, so she could climb out on the roof and hose it down, too. The roof was made of red tile, and although Abby wondered if hosing it was really necessary, she offered to help her. Then Sy'rai began hauling hoses into the house and up the stairs while Abby hooked more together.

When the trucks loaded with antiques and paintings were ready to leave, Kinky told her it was time for her to go. Joanne was sitting in the front of one of the pickups holding Vanilla in her arms.

"Leo told me to wait for him here."

"Nobody's heard from Leo in more than an hour. His last order was for me to see about you. Why don't you get in with Joanne."

"I'm staying until he comes."

"Hell, girl. Only really stubborn fools like me and Sy'rai are staying to fight to save the house or die trying. Caesar's ghost would haunt me forever if this old place burned just 'cause I ran off and left it."

"I'm staying, too."

"You've got nothing invested here. We're family."

The way he said the word *family* made her feel jealous.

"Leo's out there! Would he leave if I were out there, and he were here?"

"He wants you safe."

"He told me to stay."

"Funny, you don't seem like the obedient type." Kinky glared at her, trying to stare her down, but she squared her shoulders and folded her arms across her breasts. A full minute passed before he finally shrugged and glanced away.

"There's nothing worse than a stubborn woman," he finally said. A grim smile touched his black-rimmed lips as he glanced toward Sy'rai, who was yanking on a hose. "I should know. Hell, I've been married to one damn near my whole life. Grab a hose then before Sy'rai has a heart attack. Help her spray the Spur Tree and the grass around it."

"The Spur Tree?"

"Over there! On the other side of that far road. It's the puny-assed mesquite with all the spurs dangling off it."

Kinky turned to a couple of cowboys. "Guys, we need a firebreak around the house. Fast!"

Dark, black clouds billowed from the south where Leo was. The smoke was thickening, burning her nostrils and lungs.

"Leo," Abby whispered as she ran toward the tree that was covered with sparkling spurs, dragging a hose behind her.

Seven

Half a mile ahead Leo saw a wall of flame and clouds of black smoke. Behind that was the Big House. The loss of the old Black Oaks homestead was still fresh on his mind. The Big House appeared to be square in the middle of the fire…or gone. He couldn't tell yet.

They'd almost saved Black Oaks.

But almost didn't count. Maybe he didn't really want to know about the Big House.

Houses, even a legendary, historical house like the Big House, were just houses. Kinky would have evacuated everybody hours ago, so at least he didn't have to worry about Abby and the baby.

If he lost them… He refused to let this mind go there. He had to believe they were safe.

Leo's hair and wet clothes were singed. His muscles ached. Every sort of thorn was stuck in his skin. His eyeballs and eyelids felt dry and scratchy from too much smoke. His lungs burned.

He wanted to lie down in the road. He wanted a drink, but he kept walking, one slow, trudging step after another. Behind him, he heard Mia's leaden footsteps and her occasional whimper. She was leaning heavily on Shanghai and Cole. Leo couldn't believe Shanghai had let her fight the fire with him, but then knowing Mia, he could. She'd survived being kidnapped by a drug lord.

They say bad people go to hell when they die. Leo wasn't a damn bit sure about that. Today had taught him you didn't have to die to go to hell.

He remembered screaming "Run!" to Shanghai and Cole and Mia as the flames had swept into the oak mott surrounding the Black Oaks homestead. Blackened tree limbs had crashed around them, splintering into pieces and sending showers of sparks in all directions. One had caught Leo's shirt on fire. He could still hear the crackling wall of flames as he'd dived into the creek; he'd felt the burning limbs crashing into the water on all sides of him as the three of them had huddled under the overhang of a huge rock.

They were damn lucky to be alive. If the creek behind the homestead had been ten feet farther away or the fire faster, they never would have made it. But the flames had raced through the trees without burning all the oxygen, only half burning the branches before sweeping north toward the Big House.

Leo pictured Abby as he'd last seen her. Her eyes had been wide and so fear filled when she'd told him good-bye. He'd wanted to jump down and haul her into his arms and never let her go, but he'd known that if he'd so much as spoken to her, or touched her, he never would have been able to leave her.

Why this woman? Why her? He'd never particularly wanted to be a father again, but ever since she'd told him about the baby, he'd felt strangely protective of her. Was it solely because she was who she was, and he was an ambitious bastard? Or had she always meant more?

Abby clung to Lizzy in the humid dark of the basement that was lit by a single flashlight. A cold, deadly fear gripping her heart, Abby couldn't stop shaking.

The thick walls seemed to close in upon her. All she could think of was Leo somewhere outside in that raging inferno. If Lizzy hadn't been holding her, surely she would have gone mad.

"He has to be all right," Abby whispered. "He just has to be."

"He's a quick thinker," Lizzy said, stroking her arm. "If anybody can take care of himself out there, it's Leo."

"Do you really think so?"

"Yes."

The flashlight flickered and went out, and darkness lapped at Abby in terrifying waves. Even though her arms tightened around Lizzy, she nearly screamed. Then another beam flared, and she swallowed a shallow breath when she saw Lizzy's tremendous smile.

It seemed hours that they sat huddled together, waiting.

Then Kinky threw the lower basement door open. "You can come out! The fire's past us! We lost the garage, but the Big House is safe."

As they climbed the stairs, Lizzy said, "This room

was built to protect the family and cowboys from Native and Mexican bandit raids in the 'olden days.' Who knew we'd ever need it for a grass fire?"

Holding hands, Lizzy and Abby climbed the last of the shadowy stairs. The house was still standing. It smelled of smoke and would have to be thoroughly cleaned, of course. When they got outside and saw the scorched oaks, palms and smoldering lawn and garage, they clung to each other. As far as they could see, blackened grass stretched endlessly to the east and south.

Letting go of Lizzy, Abby's eyes had wandered from the huge mansion to the glittering spurs of the Spur Tree. A deathly quiet wrapped around her when she gazed toward the south again in the direction of Black Oaks.

Where was Leo?

Abby saw the desolation in Lizzy's eyes and sensed her concern for her husband and sister, as well. Not that either of them said anything. They were too afraid of losing control.

Abby folded Lizzy into her arms. "For now it has to be enough that the Big House and everyone who stayed here is safe."

Lizzy bit her lips. "We can still hope and pray, can't we?"

Then Kinky began shouting orders, directing them to grab shovels and throw dirt on top of hot spots. "See if we've got any water pressure. We've got some spare hoses in the basement. Get them and spray the trees again. They could still ignite."

Abby busied herself spraying the trees. A couple of hours later she was sitting on a lawn chair, wiping her brow, when she heard Kinky shouting. She looked up and saw several dirty-looking men in the distance walking up the road, waving wearily. One of the bedraggled figures was a broad-shouldered, blackened scarecrow of a man, his shirt hanging in strips against his tall, lean body. He looked tired and footsore as he shuffled across the burned grasses toward her.

"Abby!" The man's deep voice was hoarse and strange, but it made the hair on the back of her neck stand up. She felt a new alertness, a lessening of her exhaustion. There was something about his walk, something about the set of his wide shoulders.

Her heart began to throb fiercely. Her hand went to her throat. When she tried to stand, her knees buckled, and she had to push herself off the ground with her free hand.

Then Lizzy screamed Cole's name and ran past her and flung her arms around two of the scarecrow's companions.

"Leo?" Abby whispered in a breathless croak that didn't sound a bit like her voice. She felt tears on her cheeks. *"Leo!"*

Abby's pulse leaped, then stopped and then sped up again. She felt sick to her stomach, and she was afraid she'd faint. Leo started running. She sprang to her feet and flew across the yard, hurling herself into his arms.

He winced when she grabbed his back, and she said, "I'm sorry. So sorry." But his grip was still strong as he snuggled her against the long length of his body and bent his dirty face to hers. His kiss was urgent and hot, demanding and devouring. His chin was rough against the softness of hers. He tasted of soot and grime and the brush country.

She didn't care. She framed his filthy face in her palms. He was alive. His mouth was vital, and his kisses filled her with a warm, surging tide of sheer desire and wild joy.

He released her so abruptly, she would have stumbled backward if he hadn't seized her by the arms. "What the hell are you still doing here?" he growled. Then he cursed vividly.

"Shh. The baby might hear. You did tell me to wait for you."

His dark eyes glittered with anger. For long minutes his fingers ground bruisingly into the flesh of her upper arms. "Right, blame me. You little fool, don't you know you could have died?"

"But I didn't, so there's no reason to get so mad."

"No reason? The baby could have—"

"What about you? You scared me, too. Do you think I could leave, knowing you were still out there?"

Something in her expression must have gotten through to him because his harsh face softened ever so slightly.

"Abby… Abby…" He lowered his voice to a soothing purr and cupped her chin with his fingers. "Oh, Abby…"

He crooked his head and kissed her again, gently, tenderly, until her fingers were curled against his chest. He held her as she had dreamed of being held, as if he never wanted to let her go. In that moment she was so happy it was hard to remember that the thought of loving and being loved scared her more than anything.

The early-morning sky was a cerulean blue as Abby, Lizzy and Leo stood in front of the Spur Tree.

"I'm going to miss you," Lizzy said. "Except for that one other visit, I've only known you—what—a day or two, but already you seem almost like a sister."

Abby thought of Becky running away from her down that desert trail in El Paso so long ago. "Maybe because we've been through a lot together."

"Leo, did I tell you she helped me save the Spur Tree?" Lizzy asked.

"Only about ten times."

"I couldn't have done it without her."

As Leo watched them together, his stern face tightened.

"We were lucky," Abby said, taking his hand and trying to draw him closer.

"No, it was a miracle," Lizzy said. "We have many, many miracles to be thankful for this morning."

Abby threaded her fingers through Leo's. He was alive, and so were Mia, Shanghai and Cole. The Big House was still standing, and this morning six brand-new flags hung limply from its wide roof. *The six flags of Texas.* The ranch had survived one hundred forty years of Native raids, war, drought, debt and now fire.

Maybe Lizzy was right. Maybe it was a miracle. The wind had shifted and then had died. The flames were now under control, and a storm in the Gulf that was moving toward shore promised rain.

"There's something we have to do before you and Leo can leave," Lizzy said. "Close your eyes, Abby, and then open your right hand."

With quiet excitement tingling inside her, Abby smiled. "I feel like I'm eight, playing a game with Becky."

Leo's face tightened.

"Becky?" Lizzy asked.

"My twin." Abby explained.

"Now hold your hand out," Lizzy ordered as imperiously as Becky might have.

Something heavy and spiky jingled in Abby's hand.

"You can open your eyes," Lizzy said softly.

Abby gasped. "Why, they're spurs. Thank you. I'll treasure them."

"Oh, you're not going to keep them. You see, since you're leaving us, they're for the tree. We have a tradition here that's nearly one hundred and forty years old."

Lizzy touched a pair of spurs dangling from the tree and made them tinkle. "These are my daddy's spurs." Her hand touched a second pair. "And these are Uncle Jack's. Every time a cowboy who's worked the ranch dies or quits, we hang his spurs here. When people like you, who've been important to the ranch, leave, we hang his—or in your case, her—spurs on the tree, as well. Even Leo keeps a pair on the tree when he's in San Antonio."

Abby's hand closed over the spurs in her hand. "Why...why, thank you, Lizzy."

"My real mother's are hanging on the tree, too."

"But isn't Joanne..."

Lizzy shook her head. "Joanne was pregnant with Mia by Uncle Jack when she married my father. The woman Daddy loved was pregnant with me. A horse threw Uncle Jack, and he died. Electra, my real mother, wouldn't marry Daddy. So Joanne and Daddy pretended that Joanne was pregnant with twins. That way they could raise Mia and me as twins. In fact, we didn't know until a little while ago that we're really cousins, not sisters. I didn't know that my biological mother was really a woman named Electra Scott."

"The famous photojournalist? Joanne told me about her."

"Did she? Well, good, maybe she's at peace with Electra at last. They were best friends once."

"She said Leo is looking for your dad's missing daughters."

"My sisters. Joanne was pretty torn up about them when she first read Electra's journal and found out that Daddy had resumed his affair with Electra after she and Daddy were married."

Leo shifted his weight restlessly from one foot to the other. His mouth was thin, his cheeks darkly flushed. He seemed extremely edgy all of a sudden.

"So how's that investigation coming, Leo?"

A muscle flexed in his hard jawline. "What?"

"So—are there any new clues about the missing twins?"

"Maybe a few." He dropped Abby's hand and took a step backward. "Are you two ever going to hang the spurs on the damn tree or not?"

"Hey, are you okay, Leo?" Abby whispered.

"You said five minutes. The jet is waiting."

"Go on then," Abby said. "I'll just be a minute."

He hesitated, obviously skeptical. Then he pivoted on his heel and strode toward the landing strip.

"Men," Lizzy said. "Cole can be so impatient sometimes. But I've never seen Leo like this. He's usually so calm and controlled."

"He's tired. He could have been killed yesterday. We were at the emergency room half the night. I guess it's understandable."

"He's okay?"

"Except for a few cuts and bruises. Smoke inhalation, too. And he seems unusually irritable all of a sudden.

But like you said, we have a lot of miracles to be thankful for."

"You'd better hurry then. If ever a man needed a good night's sleep and a lot of TLC from his bride… You didn't have much of a honeymoon, did you?"

"No. At least, not yet…." Abby felt her cheeks heat.

Last night they'd slept together, but they'd both been so exhausted that they'd fallen asleep the minute they'd lain down in their third-floor guest room despite the fact that it had reeked of smoke. When she'd awakened, Leo's side of the bed had been empty. He'd left without a word or a kiss or any show of affection. She'd found him downstairs in the kitchen talking to Kinky and the cowboys.

Not wanting to dwell on the lack of romance last night or to keep Leo waiting, Abby held her spurs up and approached the tree, where dozens more twinkled.

Finally, after studying every branch and reading the engravings on several spurs, she hung hers on the thick branch right beside Caesar's.

Leo was striding purposefully across blackened ground and had made it halfway to the runway when his cell phone vibrated in his shirt pocket. Impatiently, he jammed it against his ear.

"How's it going down there?" Connor asked. He'd called several times, and they'd talked. He'd been watching the news, so he was up on things for the most part.

"Great. When we evacuated the ranch, Abby stayed. She helped save the Big House and the Spur Tree. Hell, she's the heroine of the hour. The family loves her."

"*Her* family. I'd say that's real, real good."

"Lizzy just gave her an honorary pair of spurs. As I

speak, she's about to hang her spurs on the same tree as her father's."

"You'd better tell who the hell she is then. And fast."

"I'd like to make sure she's on my side first."

"Always looking out for yourself, aren't you, big brother?"

"I'm real short on patience this morning. Real short."

"I can understand that after what you've been through. I don't want to get all sappy on you, but you had me going there for a while yesterday when nobody knew where you were and I saw those body bags on TV. I have to admit I said a prayer or two."

"Illegals crossing the ranch."

"Poor bastards. You know, it might help if you asked Abby about Becky. Maybe you could get her talking about the kid's hobbies and dreams. You never know…it might help me find her."

Leo grimaced. The thought of grilling Abby about her sister made him feel even guiltier than he'd felt the night he'd stolen the DNA sample from her before sleeping with her.

"All right," Leo agreed.

"Good. I gotta go, but before I do, I'll say it one more time. First chance you get, tell her."

"Hey, maybe you're my only brother, but sometimes when you stick your nose in my business, you can be a real pain in the ass."

"What's a brother for?"

Leo flipped his phone shut.

Tell her? The thought scared the hell out of him. What if he lost her?

Eight

Abby's nose was pressed against the jet's window. The sky was bright and cloudless, and the fields beneath her were abnormally brown as the jet approached the outskirts of San Antonio.

Leo, his head bent over a ledger Kinky had given him, had scarcely spoken a word on the flight. Every time Abby had even glanced his way, she'd imagined that his square jaw tensed and that his gaze narrowed.

Why was he deliberately ignoring her?

Was something bothering him? Was it something she'd done? Did he feel trapped by their marriage? He'd been so cool and controlled last night in their bedroom. Did he regret…

Stop with the negative questions. You'll drive yourself crazy. It's not like you wanted to marry him.

They'd been married all of two days. He'd barely

touched her, but somehow she felt bound to him, tuned into him on deep, unconscious levels.

What was wrong? Considering all he'd been through, he'd seemed friendly and normal enough this morning. Until Lizzy had taken them out to the Spur Tree and had handed her those damn spurs. But why would he care if Lizzy had honored her in such a way? He couldn't be jealous because the Kembles seemed to like her. But if it wasn't that, then what?

Thinking of Lizzy and the spurs made her think of Caesar's missing twin daughters. She knew Leo was conscientious to a fault. She knew he felt responsible for the fire. Lizzy had asked him about the twins. Did he feel as guilty about not having found them as she felt because Becky had never been found? Apparently he'd been looking for them for quite a while.

"I hope you don't feel bad because you haven't found Lizzy's sisters," she whispered. She thought about Becky, who'd vanished without a trace. She, of all people, knew the frustration of trying to find a missing person.

He hissed in a deep breath but didn't look up. That telltale muscle tensed in his jaw. She had the distinct impression that he definitely didn't want to talk about Lizzy's missing sisters.

"You'll find them," she said reassuringly.

He swallowed. "I'm tired, okay?"

"Of course. I understand." But she didn't look away.

"Connor's responsible for finding them. I imagine it's on his conscience more than on mine." As if to put an end to their discussion, Leo flipped a page of the ledger loudly and lowered his head over the large book.

"What happened to them? Why is it so difficult to find them?"

He slammed the ledger, and she knew he wished she'd leave him alone. Well, it had been his idea to marry. Maybe it was time he learned that if they were stuck together, she couldn't stand the silent treatment.

"Leo, I asked you why it was so difficult—"

"I heard you, okay?" He drew a long breath. "Look, Electra was famous, and so was Caesar. She didn't want to damage Caesar's marriage, so she was very secretive when she put them up for adoption. She used an agency that agreed to a closed adoption. As a result, getting those records has been extremely difficult and time-consuming."

"But you got them?"

His mouth thinned. He nodded. "But often when two people adopt in a situation like that, they're secretive, too," he said. "Maybe they don't ever intend to tell their children they're adopted. And since the girls would be…er…in their twenties now…"

"You said they were nearly twenty-seven. My age."

He swallowed again.

"Right," he said. "People in their twenties move around a lot. They could be anywhere."

"So, Connor's really, really good at finding missing people?"

"That's what he does."

"You know, I have a missing sister, too. Do you think maybe I could talk to him about her sometime? We lost her when she was eight. Ever since then, it's like a part of my soul is still missing."

He grabbed a decanter of scotch from a low table and

poured himself a glass, which he gulped in a single long swallow. "That's awful," he replied.

"We're twins, too. That's sort of a strange coincidence, don't you think?"

"What? You are? Right! Yes, it is! Damn right it is!"

"Becky, that's my sister who disappeared when she was eight," Abby persisted. "I loved her, and I still miss her. I still wonder if she's alive...if she's happy...if she remembers me."

"I'm sorry," he said. He took her hand is his. "Look, I'm really sorry about her." The jet hit an air pocket just as the blood rushed from his face. He was as pale as a ghost, and his eyes blazed queerly. When she squeezed his hand to reassure him, he jumped. Then the jet hit real turbulence, and his stare became so wild and intense that she sucked in a panicky breath. "What? Is...is something wrong with the jet?"

"No. Just a bit of bumpy air. Sorry if I scared you. See...the jet's leveling out. Nothing's wrong."

"It's such a coincidence, me being the same age as the missing twins...and me having a missing twin."

"Yes, I suppose it is." He took a deep breath as if he were choosing carefully what he intended to say. Then he stopped, shook his head and closed his eyes for a long moment. He took two long breaths, and when he opened his eyes again, she was relieved that he seemed almost his old, assured self. Then he ran his hand through his heavy, black hair, she saw that he had a slight tremor.

She felt profound sympathy for him. It must be the turbulence. She hadn't realized he was such a nervous flyer. Maybe he wasn't usually, but he'd been through a lot. Obviously, he wanted to appear tough and unruffled.

He met her gaze. "You say your twin is missing? How did it happen? When?"

Abby didn't want to upset him. Not when he was this worried about flying. Still, he seemed so concerned and interested, that suddenly she couldn't stop herself.

"We were eight," she began in a breathless rush. "We'd been making too much noise in the tent where we were camping in the Franklin Mountains in El Paso, so our parents had made us go outside. We were playing this silly game, chasing each other and hiding from one another. Then we ran after a wild turkey. When the sun began going down, I suddenly realized how far we were from the tent, so I turned to run back down the hill. Becky yelled for me to wait… But I didn't, even though she sounded terrified."

"And?"

"I thought she would follow me like she always did. She was more afraid of the dark than I was, you see. Oh, why am I telling you all this, when you already have way too much on your mind?"

"Because I asked." His voice was low and soothing.

"I never saw her again," she whispered. "Nobody did."

Leo took her hand in his, and his tense, dark eyes shone with compassion. That's when the worst of the pain that she'd carried inside her for years and years burst forth.

"My father thought it was his fault. He'd been down in Mexico just before that, writing about stuff powerful people didn't want exposed. He thinks she was taken across the border. But I knew it was my fault. If I hadn't run away and left her, maybe she wouldn't have gotten lost. And maybe my parents wouldn't have gotten divorced. Maybe Mother wouldn't have died. And maybe I wouldn't have dated all those cowboys who could never have loved me. I didn't want them to love me, you see. Not even Shanghai. Because then they'd leave me. And maybe if I hadn't run away from her that day, my father would do things with me. Like, for instance, maybe he would have come to our wedding." She felt like a fool when she sobbed out that last.

"Shh. You're being way too hard on yourself." He yanked a tissue out of a little box from the nearby table and handed it to her. "Here. Blow your nose."

"T-this is…is why I never talk about her," she sobbed. "Why I try to never think about her." More hot tears fell. "B-because i-it upsets me too much. She was scared, and I left her out there in the dark all alone. And…and I can't stop wondering what happened to her. All this talk about the missing twins has stirred me up I think."

Abby felt weak and exhausted and absolutely raw after her tearful outburst. Fighting the fire was nothing compared to talking about Becky. She sat back, drained.

"I see." Leo's thoughtful gaze studied her. "A while ago you asked about talking to my brother." He seemed to consider his words. "Maybe you should phone Connor and tell him everything you know about Becky. *Everything*."

"It's been such a long time. I hardly dare to hope that even he can find—"

"Hopefully, he'll surprise us," Leo muttered gloomily. His grip on her hand tightened, and she wondered why he suddenly sounded so morose and hopeless again.

As if sensing she was worried, his arm came

around her, and his touch was so soothing she loosened her seat belt so she could curl up against him. She wished he would keep talking to her, because she'd liked sharing with him about Becky, but he said no more.

Instead, a heavy silence fell between them. His body felt tense and hard. Soon she realized an even thicker wall had gone up, a wall that she had no idea how to tear down. Why was he so quiet and uncommunicative all of a sudden when he'd been so attentive after that first night she'd slept with him? Before they'd married, he'd wanted to see her again constantly. Only minutes ago he'd listened to what she'd shared about Becky, but now he was shutting her out again.

"Leo? Are you okay? Did I say something or do something…"

"I'm fine. Just tired."

His tension seemed to increase. After they landed, he drove them in silence to her ranch house, stopping briefly to buy groceries. Without a word he pulled up to her back porch and unloaded their bags and the food. Then he told her he had a lot to catch up on. He called his office and stayed on the phone with various people for hours. She spoke to Kel briefly. Five minutes was all it took for her to catch up on things at In the Pink! When Leo remained in her second bedroom with his phone, she prepared and ate a cold supper of cottage cheese, carrot sticks and sardines—alone. As she'd done on their wedding night, she bathed and brushed her hair until it gleamed. She put on her sheerest nightgown and left her robe seductively unfastened, but when he finally came to bed, dressed only in his pajama bottoms, he gave her a light peck on the cheek. Then he rolled over to his side of the bed, turned his broad, powerful back to her and was silent.

Blinking back tears, she glared at him.

Why didn't he try to seduce her as he had the night he'd proposed?

"Leo?"

He stirred. "Hmm?"

"Is something wrong?"

"I'm just tired," he whispered. "Go to sleep."

She was a new bride. They'd both come close to death. She'd sat in that basement, terrified he was dead. She wanted him to wrap her in his arms, to make wild, violent love to her. But she would not beg.

Go to sleep?

As if she could.

The bloodred neon of the alarm clock was blinking 2:00 a.m. when Abby's breathing finally slurred to a soft and regular rhythm. At last, Leo thought. Maybe soon, he'd be able to fall asleep, too. God knew, he'd better.

He'd known by her choice of nightgown—the damn thing left nothing to his imagination—that she'd wanted him. Just as he'd known by her crushed tone that he'd hurt her when he'd kissed her coolly and turned his back on her. He'd lain there, his heart pounding with desire while his mind was tormented by guilt.

It had taken her hours to fall asleep. Leo knew because he'd been driven crazy by the blinking clock and by her fidgeting.

Asleep now, she snuggled closer to him, her delicious warmth invading his side of the bed. God. He bit his lower lip and turned to stare at her slim body molded by the quilts beside his.

In the moonlight, her loose, butter-gold hair gleamed like silk on the pillow. His heartbeat sped up.

He wanted to touch her hair, to thread his fingers through it, to kiss it, just as he wanted to brush her pale throat with his mouth. He craved her smell, her satiny softness, her taste. He'd wanted all those things last night, too, but he knew just as he'd known last night, that if he so much as held her hand, he wouldn't be able to stop. His deception and sex had gotten them off to the wrong start, and only honesty would set things right. But was she ready for the brutal truth? He'd known who she was, and he'd set her up.

Leo swallowed. Surely lying beside Abby without touching her, knowing she was awake and as needily restless as he, had been the cruelest of tortures. He'd lain there, remembering the fear blazing in her hazel eyes when she'd walked up to Kinky's SUV before they'd headed out to Black Oaks. Nor could he forget the wild joy in her eyes when she'd realized he'd survived. He'd never forget how she'd flown into his arms after the fire had passed the house.

Nobody could fake such emotions. Her heart and soul had been in that kiss. So had his.

If anything, his feelings were even stronger than hers, maybe because he'd lived most of his life in such a cold place. Ever since that moment in front of the Big House, he'd known he cared for her more than he'd ever imagined possible.

When he'd been in the thick of those flames at Black Oaks, fighting the fire and then fighting for his own life, she and the baby had held an inexplicable, almost mythical power over him. He'd wanted to live, solely to get back to them. He'd wanted a chance to be Abby's lover, her husband and the father of their child.

He'd prayed for a miracle as he'd dived into the creek as the trees on all sides of him had exploded in flames. Then he'd seen Abby again, and she'd kissed him so fiercely in that blackened pasture, he'd almost thought he could have his miracle. But his wild hope had made him more afraid.

How could he trust her not to break his heart when she learned the truth? Somehow he had to figure out a way to win her—permanently. Because if he lost her now, he knew from past experience how unbearable such pain would be. When he'd lost Ransom's respect and support, and Nancy and Julie and his mother, he'd lived in a bleak, lonely place fueled only by the cold brilliance of his ambition.

It had been a long, ruthless climb up from his hellish losses. So he didn't have the guts to face losing Abby. He had to calm down and woo her slowly, deliberately.

Ignoring difficult conversations wasn't going to work very long. He had to talk to her, confide in her, listen to her. But not tonight.

In a few months, after he'd won her trust, maybe then he'd find the courage to tell her everything. He could only hope that by then he would have proved he cared and she'd have enough invested in their relationship to forgive him.

In her dream, Leo was cupping her breasts and kissing her endlessly. Then something screamed outside the window, the owls maybe, rudely awakening her. The next thing she grew aware of was Leo's steady breathing.

Slowly she realized that Leo was on his side of the bed—as far away from her as possible. He lay on his back with his arms crossed. His eyes were open, and he was staring up at the ceiling.

He was awake.

"Leo?" Abby whispered, reaching for him before she thought.

His reaction to her lush voice and caressing fingertips was instantaneous and undeniable. As he grabbed her hand and stilled it against his abdomen, his breath caught in his throat. She could tell by the sheet bunched at his groin that he was hard, erect. His skin was burning hot, and his heart was pounding as fiercely as hers.

He wanted her, every bit as much as she wanted him. Yet he was pretending not to.

"Go back to sleep," he growled, pushing her hand away. Then he rolled to the very edge of his side of the bed and lay facing the far wall.

Why was he rejecting her? She should respect his wishes, shouldn't she? And she would, if only he would tell her why.

"Leo…did I do something…?"

"No, I said—"

"But I'm not sleepy."

"Well, I am," Leo said.

"Are you? I wonder."

Her dream made her bold. Giggling, she scooted beneath the sheets until her soft breasts grazed the warmth of his broad back. Her nipples grew hard the instant she felt his smooth, hot flesh. He hissed in a breath, tensing when she stayed there with her breasts mashed against his back. For a second she thought he might jump from the bed. Just to tempt him, she slid her hand down his side to rest upon his buttocks. Gently, slowly, her fingers kneaded.

"I want you," she whispered finally, splaying her fingertips. "I want you so much."

Her hand traced back up the length of his side with exquisite tenderness. He turned, caught her hand and kissed it. Then he went still, slowly he pushed her away, sprang out of the bed and went to the window, where he stood, fists clenched at his sides.

"Leo?"

He sucked in a harsh breath and stayed where he was.

She punched her pillow in frustration. "All right," she finally said. Getting up, she threw on her robe and walked down the hall into her kitchen. Closing the door, she pulled out a chair. Sitting down at the table, she buried her head in her hands.

Did he hate her? Hate himself for desiring her? He'd been so sweet and understanding on the plane when she'd told him about Becky. If he didn't hate her, what was wrong now?

She thought of their child. Did he feel trapped as she had? She wished her dream hadn't made her so brazen. Her stomach tightened.

Why had she touched him, pushed him? Like her, he was used to being in charge. How could she have been so conceited as to think she could seduce him when he was set against her? Why hadn't she given him the time he needed? He'd been through a lot…the news of her pregnancy, their rushed marriage, the fire, blaming himself for all of it, probably. Then she'd pushed him about the missing twins on the plane.

She began to berate herself as being the most selfish, pushy person ever. She didn't know him that well. He was used to his own space. She needed to slow down, to be careful for a while.

He'd been injured in the fire. Last night he'd been in the emergency room. He was probably still exhausted. Maybe he was in pain.

Scalding tears slipped from her eyelids. He'd probably despise her forever now.

Her sobs blocked the sound of his soft tread, so she didn't realize he was anywhere near until he said her name.

When she looked up, he towered over her. He was still bare-chested, wearing only his pajama bottoms.

He knelt and pulled her into his arms. "I'm sorry."

"I'm sorry, too," she whispered as she threw her arms around his shoulders. "Oh, Leo…I-I'm so sorry."

He pressed her close, stroked her back, her hair. She clung to him and was amazed that she was so starved for any show of kindness or affection from him. Never had she wanted any man's caresses and interest as she wanted his. What were these new feelings?

He stared into her eyes for a long moment with a burning intensity that left her breathless even before he traced the back of his hand against the softness of her cheek and then down her throat.

"My precious wife. My darling…"

Her nipples tightened. She swallowed, hoping for more. Then his hand stopped moving.

"Do you hate me?" she whispered.

"God, no. How could you even think…?"

He crushed her to his chest and held her tightly. She felt the thunder of his heart, the warmth of his powerful body.

Her sobs subsided, and she clung more tightly, laying her head, cheek to cheek, against his. He was alive and so solid and strong, so dear. She liked simply being held in his arms. Her dream had not been nearly so good as this. Closing her eyes, she prayed that he would kiss her. Afraid to encourage him, she remained still and breathless in his arms, waiting.

His hand began to move up and down her back. Then he caressed her neck, her shoulders, her arms, and whispered, "Sweet. You tempt me to…"

But he did not kiss her lips or touch her breasts.

Instead, he said, "Come back to bed, my darling."

My darling. The gentle endearment chimed in her soul. *He'd called her his darling. He didn't hate her.*

Threading her fingers inside his, he led her back down the hall.

As he slid the covers back, she saw that his pajama bottoms were tented at his crotch. So, he did desire her.

When they were both in bed, he said good-night. His voice was husky, and he was shaking slightly. He wanted her as badly as she wanted him. Why was he doing this? Why wasn't he going to take her? Why?

She closed her eyes and took a deep breath, willing him to kiss her. But he didn't.

"Good night, Leo," she finally rasped.

Tears beaded her lashes as she lay in the dark, hungering for more.

"Good night," he muttered in a low, choked tone.

She lay in the dark beside him, too aware of his big, long body just inches from hers. Still, as frustrating as his nearness was, his being there made her feel safe. It wasn't long before she fell asleep, and in her dreams he clasped her to him and made love to her as ardently as she desired.

In the morning when she awoke, he was staring so with such intensity that she blushed.

She realized the sheets had come off, and in her sheer nightgown, she was practically naked.

"What?" she whispered, smiling at him because she felt exposed and liked the way his hot eyes burned through the thin fabric to her skin.

"Sleep well?" His voice was gruff and tight.

She sighed. Then she stretched, just to tempt him. "Never better."

He didn't yield; his eyes remained glued to her face. Was he afraid to look at her body in the revealing nightgown? She could see his pulse knocking in the hollow of his tanned throat. She hoped so.

"Did you know you cried out my name...several times?" he said.

"I must have been having a nightmare."

"Didn't sound like it to me."

"Oh, really?" She got up and threw her pillow at him. Without bothering to throw on her robe or cover herself, she scampered off to her bathroom and locked the door. Not that it was necessary. She'd locked it solely to taunt him.

The heat of his gaze had seared through her nightgown. Maybe he hadn't wanted to stare at her, but he hadn't been able to look away. Once she was safe inside, she leaned against the door for a long time, trembling.

Where did she go from here?

Nine

Later that morning, to Abby's surprise, Leo had supervised the high-school kid he'd hired to see to Coco and had scrambled eggs and cooked bacon by the time she'd showered and dressed. He'd hauled out the garbage, as well.

Now he was dressed in dark slacks, a white shirt and tie. His dark jacket hung over a kitchen chair, and his bulging black briefcase stood by the door.

"You're fast and capable and handy to have around," she said as she sat down at the table on her back porch that he'd set. "I'll give you that."

"Hey, who knows, maybe you'll decide I'm a keeper. Beautiful morning," he murmured as he unfolded his napkin.

Sunlight slanted through the oaks and pines. Birds twittered in their branches.

"Yes."

Why were his knuckles white as he held his fork? Why was his face so hard and set? She'd barely slept. Maybe he was as tired as she was.

They ate in silence. When they were done, he stacked their plates and headed into the kitchen. Obviously in a rush, he began rinsing and putting the dishes into the dishwasher.

"I'll be home at seven," he said when he'd finished. "What's your schedule?"

"It'll probably be pretty hectic, but I'll try to be here by seven, too."

His smiled. "Good. We can cook or go out, whatever you'd prefer."

"You're being so agreeable."

"Why is that such a surprise?"

Remembering his rejection last night, she looked up, but his dark, smiling eyes were unreadable.

He went to the door and picked up his briefcase. Hoping he would kiss her goodbye, she chased after him. Instead, he turned and nodded. Then he said shortly, "See you—"

See you. She was a new bride. They'd missed their honeymoon, and he was treating her like a sister.

He pushed the screen door open. Feeling forlorn, she ran after him and watched from the porch when he drove away.

All through the day, she found herself hurrying to get finished with her phone calls and even her pet projects so that she'd make it home to him at the stroke of seven. And when she did make it, by recklessly speeding, and five whole minutes early, her heart fell when his truck wasn't there.

Thirty minutes later he called and said he'd be home at eight.

"I'll have dinner ready."

"Not sardines and carrots, I hope."

She laughed. "No. Steak and potatoes and green beans and chocolate cookies with ice cream. Store-bought, I'm afraid."

"Maybe you're a keeper, too."

"You think?"

"I think. Let me get back to this so I can get home." The eagerness in his low voice warmed her heart.

That night he brought her a box of chocolates and a single red rose. Not that he kissed her at the door or anything, even though she'd come running as soon as she'd heard his truck.

Sexual tension thrummed in her blood as she found a vase and stuck the rose in it. With shaking fingers, she set the vase on the table. All through dinner she found herself turning from his dark face to the rose and wondering why he'd bought it when he wouldn't even kiss her.

After supper they took a walk with Coco following them as the sky turned violet and stars popped out. Leo told her about his day, which had been every bit as crazy as hers, and she told him amusing stories about her meetings and unreasonable clients. He smiled and laughed a lot, and she was aware of him watching her when he thought she wasn't looking.

How could she have ever thought him dull when just being with him around the house was fun? Not since she'd had Becky around had she had someone to share the little things that made up her life. She'd thought he couldn't possibly be interested in hearing about one client's fit over naming and marketing ideas for a new product, but he was either fascinated and held her talent in awe, or he deserved an Oscar.

When it was dark and the moon had come up, they returned to the house and watched part of an old black-and-white Western on television. He confessed he was a sucker for all John Wayne movies.

"I guess in my heart I always dreamed of being a cowboy," he admitted.

"I'm a sucker for anything with a horse in it, too," she said. "A book, a movie…"

He was attentive from the moment he got home until they went to bed. They did nothing out of the ordinary, but the evening was special in so many ways, at least for her, as only simple pleasures can be special when shared with a friend or lover. Was that what he was doing—trying to become her friend?

But again, when they went to bed, he kept to his own side of the bed. Only tonight he didn't even kiss her on the cheek.

Why didn't he push for sex? She quit asking. She decided to try to be patient. Thus, a week passed in this pleasant if frustrating fashion, and with each new day the sexual tension inside her built. Every night he was a perfect friend, a perfect gentleman, but never her lover except in her dreams.

When Connor flew to Austin Friday afternoon to meet a client, Leo set up a late-afternoon appointment for Abby to meet him in her office to discuss Becky. As always, she promised Leo she'd be home at seven. When Connor didn't make it to her office until six, she didn't think to call Leo and warn him. She was so anxious about the interview, she simply shook hands with Connor, closed her office door and turned her cell phone to silent, so they wouldn't be interrupted.

"Sorry I'm late," he said grinning. "Airport. Airplane. Client."

"Say no more. Would you like something to drink?"

"Just water. Lots of ice."

By the time she returned to her desk with two bottles and two glasses of ice, he had his laptop up and running.

He asked all the same questions about Becky she'd answered too many times before, and as always, as he entered her replies into his laptop, she tensed and hunched over, her head pounding.

"What did Becky want to be when she grew up?"

Abby closed her eyes. If she grew up. "A teacher. But she was only eight. How many of us know at that age?" Funny, how she always thought of Becky as eight…as if her life had stopped…Abby's throat tightened.

"Did she like horses, too?"

"No, she was scared of them. Our horse, Blacky, stepped on her big toe and broke it, and she wouldn't go near the barn after that."

"What else was she scared of?"

"Mostly the dark. Snakes. Bugs, especially scorpions. All the usual suspects little girls are afraid of. Goblins under the bed. Disney villains like the witch in *Snow White*. Oh, and the tooth fairy. We always left our teeth under my pillow."

Connor smiled. "Was there anything unusual about her, anything at all that set her apart?"

"She was very sensitive, unusually compassionate.

She would always notice if anybody's feelings were hurt and try to comfort them."

As they talked, Abby lost track of the time. It was almost seven-thirty when Connor said he thought he had enough to go on.

"But do you really think there's a chance that you might find her?"

"Maybe. But you've got to understand that this case is very cold."

Feeling weary from all the emotions his questions had stirred, she nodded. Without another word, she got up and walked him to the door.

He insisted on following her down to her Lincoln. "Are you staying at the Little Spur or in town?" she asked as she flung her purse and briefcase onto her passenger seat and then sank behind the wheel.

"Neither. I'm flying back to Houston tonight."

"Thanks for looking into this."

"No. Thank you." He shook her hand.

Her mind whirled with memories about Becky as she drove home. Connor seemed cocky, but she was afraid to hope.

She was still thinking about Becky as she drove into the garage. No sooner had she gotten out of the Lincoln than Leo ran out of the house. He looked tall and strong and handsome in snug-fitting, faded jeans and a long-sleeved white shirt as he waited for her in the drive. His black hair fell loosely over his tanned brow. She wanted him to take her in his arms, to hold her. Would he never, ever kiss her again?

She drew in a long, shaky breath. Maybe part of her exhaustion had to do with her pregnancy, but she was utterly drained from her long day, the meeting about Becky and then the drive home.

"I'm sorry I'm late," she said as she wearily picked up her briefcase.

He stood in the dark, silently watching her.

"Is something wrong?" she whispered when his silence began to grow heavy.

"Where have you been? I tried and tried to call...."

"You called? Me?"

"You. I sent a text message, too."

She fumbled in her purse for her cell phone and saw that he had. "Oh, I—I guess I turned it to silent ring when I was in that meeting with Connor. Yes, I did."

"You scared the hell out of me."

"Oh, Leo, I-I'm sorry."

She could tell he was upset. His lips were pale and thinner than usual. When he pushed that lock of hair back, she saw that a vein pulsed in his forehead. Yet, the next time he spoke, his voice sounded remarkably controlled, even calm. "It's okay now that you're here, safe."

He grabbed her briefcase. "So, how'd the meeting with my brother go?" he asked as they began to walk to the house.

"He asked me so many questions. Talking about Becky made me so tense I have a headache and a backache."

"I was afraid. I imagined all sorts of wild scenarios. A flat...your Lincoln spinning out of control...a wreck...you hurt..."

He certainly didn't sound like an indifferent husband.

"Oh, dear. Leo, the last thing I wanted to do was upset you."

"I wasn't upset," he said, but his teeth were tightly clenched.

"Why were you so worried?"

"Break in routine, I guess. Let's forget it."

His strides became so long and quick, she had to run to keep up with him. He wasn't dull or cold. His emotions were fierce and all-consuming. Tonight she needed passion.

She needed to be kissed and held. After talking to Connor, she was afraid she'd never see Becky again. After the interview had ended, all she'd wanted was to get home to Leo. She'd imagined his arms around her, longed for them. Tonight she wanted Leo the lover, not Leo the friend.

When she stepped into the kitchen, he had a pasta dish ready to serve. She knew she was being thoughtless and selfish, but she wasn't in the mood for one of their friendly evenings.

"You know what I really need tonight, Leo?"

He turned and glanced past her. Sparks lit her blood. Not that he met her gaze.

She felt awful chasing him, but she couldn't stop herself. "I—I feel as if tension has settled in every nerve and muscle and ligament. If I weren't pregnant, I'd have a beer or a glass of wine. I'll never be able to relax unless I take a warm bath and maybe…maybe, if you wouldn't mind, you could massage me a little."

He closed his eyes and clenched his fists. "Not a good idea."

She shouldn't—she wouldn't—beg him.

Swallowing her pride, she did. "Please…"

The silent kitchen surrounded them. When he

frowned, she felt a horrible certainty that he was about
to refuse her.

"Leo. I got so upset thinking about Becky…"

"All right," he said. "You win."

"I'm ready," Abby called to him huskily.

Leo's heart was rushing way too fast as he pushed
open the door. He went still, staring at her.

He couldn't do this. But he had to.

Vanilla candles flickered, their soft glow bathing the
exposed curve of her slim back in warm, golden light.
Sheets were bunched at her rounded hips. Her hair
gleamed like dark gold. Hungrily his eyes devoured her.
All week he'd held himself in check even though he'd
lusted for her constantly. Every night her nightgowns had
seemed to grow thinner. Now, tonight, she was naked.

Soft, serene music played. A bottle of her favorite,
lavender-scented lotion stood on the bedside table.

Leo was convinced they needed more time, several
weeks maybe, to get to know each other. He had taken
a long walk, telling himself that he could massage her
without letting it go any further…that he had to.

He knew what talking about Becky did to her.
Abby was pregnant, shattered and exhausted tonight.
He kept reminding himself that they'd gone to bed
before they'd trusted each other, and how ashamed
she'd been of the dark, wild things she'd done with a
near-stranger. He wanted to become her friend, someone she trusted before he touched her again. Tonight
was too soon.

He must have made some sound because her fingers
tensed, clawing the sheets. Desire raced through his

veins and made every muscle in his being tense even as he fought it.

He went to the bed and fumbled to loosen the bottle's cap. Squirting a big blob of cold lotion into his hands much too violently, he waited awhile for it to warm.

"Leo?"

"Just heating the lotion up a bit."

"Or stalling?"

She had him there. "Sorry." He hastily knelt beside the bed and placed trembling hands on her bare shoulders.

For a long moment his hands remained still as her heat seeped into his fingers, causing his muscles to wind tighter. He sank his teeth into his bottom lip until it bled.

He couldn't do this.

"Your hands feel so good. Big and warm. I feel safe tonight with you," she murmured.

Damn. His heart was pounding like a drumbeat gone wild. He was as hard as a brick. He felt like a beast. She was naked under that sheet. Was she trying to drive him crazy or what?

Desperately, he swallowed. Then he forced his hands to move in ever-widening circular motions.

"That feels so good," she whispered huskily.

He shut his eyes, but he still saw her golden hair, the slope of her shoulders, the curve of her hips, and imagined the rest.

His breathing grew ragged. His pulse raced out of control. He wanted her so much he couldn't trust himself a second longer.

His hands stopped. For a long moment he stayed beside her, frozen.

Then she turned, the sheets falling away so that he

saw the triangular wedge of gold curls that concealed the secret of her womanhood. Her pale breasts with their shadowy nipples were uncovered to his gaze.

"Leo, I want to touch you, too. Please…please let me."

He stood up and stared down at her lush golden body, at her soft, wet, red lips. Then he ran.

"Leo?" she whispered in a tiny, bleak voice.

Every organ in Leo's body pulsed with blood and felt on fire as he stood in the guest bathroom splashing cold water onto his face and hair.

"Don't you want me at all?" she murmured from the doorway.

She was probably naked. And so close.

Hell. He stiffened. Why couldn't she just leave him alone?

When he glanced up into the mirror, he saw that her golden hair tumbled about her shoulders in wild dis-array and that she wasn't naked anymore. She was wearing a thick red robe that was tied loosely at her waist…and probably nothing else. Her mouth was trembling. Her big sad eyes were asking questions he wasn't sure how to answer. The last thing he wanted to do was to hurt her.

"I think you know I want you," he said.

"Then why have you…or maybe I should ask why haven't you…"

A dark flush crawled up her neck and stained her cheeks.

"Dammit. Because I selfishly seduced you the first night and made you hate me. Then you told me you were pregnant and miserable because of me, and I seduced you to get you to agree to marry me. I've been a bastard. Because of our sexual history, I thought that maybe we should try to become friends before we did it again."

Her face softened. "Really? You were trying to be considerate?"

He nodded.

"That's so sweet."

"Believe me, I'm the last thing from sweet."

"What if I don't choose to believe you?"

"I assure you, my motives are extremely selfish."

A huge smile lit her face. "I'm so glad." Then she laughed and came into his arms, gasping when she felt his male hardness pressing against her pelvis.

"So you do want me?" she whispered huskily. "You do!"

"I do," he murmured, ruffling her hair.

"I'm glad. Very pleased. But I want more than friendship. We're married now…you know."

He knew. His heart was pounding violently.

The bathroom shade was up. Outside, the night was velvet black with only the faintest shimmer of silver moonlight. In that strange, gray light, her normally fiery hair gleamed like platinum.

His arms tightened around her. He'd never felt so close to any woman. Not even Nancy, the girl he'd loved as a boy. And he'd thought he'd never get over Nancy.

His lips found Abby's in a long, hard kiss, his tongue plunging into her mouth. Fumbling with the tie of her robe, she yanked it loose. When she wiggled, it slid off her body. At the sight of her naked, he gripped her arms so hard she cried out.

"Sorry," he whispered. Then he began to tear off his

belt and jeans. Stepping out of the denim, he tossed his jeans aside.

He pushed her against the wall. She was wet with lotion and as slick as satin, open. He stepped back, panting hard. Beneath her long lashes, her eyes were brilliant. Her lips looked swollen and bruised. He remembered that first night when she'd been so hungry for him. Not that they'd been any hungrier for each other than they were now.

"Wrap your legs around me," he commanded roughly. Grabbing her buttocks and pulling her tight, he drove himself into her.

When he filled her the first time, he went still, and she sighed.

"Yes," she murmured. "I thought you'd never…do this…again…."

She said more, but he didn't hear the rest. Still inside her, holding her bottom tightly against his pelvis, he carried her down the hall to her bedroom. With her legs laced around his waist, he lowered her to the bed and then followed her down.

Her pleadings, or whatever the hell they were, fell against his ears in broken whispers, but his desire drove him. He was past hearing her, past everything but the insane, pulsing need that drove him to make her completely his.

Again and again he plunged, each time more forcefully, each time finding a pleasure and a satisfaction unlike any he had ever known until finally he rushed over that final edge, shuddering as he exploded. She wept, clinging, stroking, trembling.

"Did I hurt you?" he whispered.

She kissed his mouth and shook her head back and forth on her pillow. Then she touched the tip of her nose to his.

Vaguely he hoped it wasn't too soon, but he'd wanted her too much and she'd been too sweet…and too hot to resist. He was still burning up.

He'd intended to go a while longer without sex, to court her slowly, to make her like him. So much for good intentions. There were those who'd said he'd been on the road to hell since birth.

He fell asleep while still inside her, with her arms wrapped tightly around him.

Ten

When Leo awoke the next morning, streamers of pink light drifted across the bed. The window must have been cracked an inch or so because he heard wild turkeys gobbling and morning doves cooing.

Glancing at his watch, he saw it was too early to get up. When Abby whispered his name, he pulled her warm, luscious body close. Then he ran his hand down her arm, which was velvety soft and deliciously warm. He kissed the curve of her elbow where a faint pulse throbbed.

She sighed and then reached over and framed his face with her hands. He stared at her before kissing her on the lips. She opened her mouth, and his tongue dipped inside.

"Wait! I've got to get up and brush my…"

"I can't wait."

He circled her with his arms and slid on top of her,

holding her down and parting her legs. His sex found hers. She was slick wet, and so hot. Satin wildfire.

When he went still instead of entering her, he swallowed convulsively. He kissed her again and again, on her throat, on the tip of her nose, on her lips, until her skin felt feverish all over.

"Now it's me who can't wait," she teased, nipping playfully at his bottom lip.

"All right then." He lunged, and her eyes flashed open as she cried out in pleasure.

"Don't move. I want this to last," he said.

"So do I. Oh, so do I."

He tried to slow down and keep his strokes featherlight, but her body gloved him tightly, causing too many exquisite sensations to course down every male nerve ending. It was as if they were wired for each other.

He'd hungered for her too long, and the taste he'd had last night wasn't nearly enough. She moved, causing hot bursts of thrilling sensations to course through him. It wasn't long before he lost all control and began thrusting faster and faster himself. Then they were both crying out at once and holding each other, swept away in a volcanic riptide that left them shaken and yet happy, too.

When he finally got up that morning, he tiptoed from the room. Several minutes later, when he was dressed for work and sitting down to a couple of fried eggs with his newspaper, dammit if the little minx didn't crawl under the kitchen table, unzip his slacks and make him forget all about breakfast and his office. She was insatiable.

Afterward, he pulled her into his lap and told her that was the most memorable breakfast he'd ever had.

"But your eggs are cold," she teased, nuzzling her lips against his throat.

As if he gave a damn. "I'm calling Miriam to tell her I'll be very late."

"Why?" she asked, but she winked at him.

He ripped off his tie and unbuttoned his dress shirt. "Because I've got a favor or two to return. I like to stay even. Why don't you call your office and tell them you won't be in until ten? I promise you won't regret it."

After he returned the sexual favor that she had bestowed on him, she told him again how sweet she thought he was for trying to make her know he respected her.

"But really, surely you could have done that some other way. Not kissing you, not being kissed, not being held, and all the other things we didn't do, was pure torture…at least for me," she said.

"For me, too. Believe me, I sympathize. But you do remember how mad you got at me after that first night. You called me a stalker."

She blushed. "I'm sorry. I thought I had to say something awful to make you go away."

"Why were you so determined you wanted nothing to do with me?"

"I—I was afraid of you, I think. Of how you made me feel…and lose control."

"Are you still afraid?"

"More than ever."

"Because you lost Becky?"

"And my parents, too. Still, avoiding sex wasn't a very practical idea, since we seem to think about it a lot when we're together."

"You can say that again."

"How long did you intend to stay celibate?"

"I don't know," he said. "A few more weeks. I thought maybe we should get to know each other a little better before—"

"But we're married," she murmured. "Hey, do you think we could stay home today?"

"And do what?"

"Are you going to make me keep chasing you?"

In the end, they stayed home all day. Leo told Miriam since he'd skipped his honeymoon, he deserved to spend one day with his bride. And Miriam, bless her practical, capable heart, didn't put up a single argument. The woman she'd once disliked was becoming one of her favorite people.

Bliss-filled days and nights became the norm for Leo and Abby.

They spent the Fourth of July at the headquarters of the Golden Spurs. It had rained, and except for the scarred trees, much of the damage to the pastures from the fire was brightened by leafy new foliage. Fences had been repaired and buildings were being reconstructed.

The Kembles made a fuss over her and her growing belly. It was funny how she felt so close to Mia and Lizzy. She liked to hang out in the barn with Mia and her horses or just sit and chat with Lizzy. It was strange how easily she got along with the Kemble sisters.

Although the summer was long and hot, and the drought, especially in South Texas was a fierce one, Abby felt happier than she'd ever been.

Not that life was perfect. Despite her frequent conversations with Connor and his determination to find her sister, Becky's disappearance remained a mystery. Nor had her father called or answered her e-mails once since their wedding. It was as if after he'd called to say he wasn't coming to her wedding, he'd disappeared off the face of the earth.

"He doesn't care about me," Abby said to Leo one evening in early September as he lay on the couch, perusing some papers from his briefcase that had to do with a pending oil and gas lease on the Golden Spurs.

"He cares," Leo said. "He just doesn't know how to show it. Sometimes when you're running from the crap in your life you can't face, you bury yourself alive in your work so you don't hate yourself. I should know. I did that for years after Mike Ransom threw me off his ranch. Do you remember that day you came to my office to tell me you were pregnant?"

"As if I could ever forget it."

He smiled. "Do you remember that old man who left when you came in?"

She nodded. "The skinny old gentleman who called you a bastard?"

"My mother worked on the Running R, his ranch, as his housekeeper when I was a kid. My father was dead, so Ransom became like a father to Connor and me. He invited us everywhere he took his own son, Cal. Took us to football games and theater road shows in Dallas. Taught us to ride, shoot and rope. Hell, he was even our Scout leader. I grew up loving him like a father."

"What happened?"

"Cal and I both fell in love with Nancy, a neighboring rancher's daughter. She chose me over Cal even though he was rich, and I was poor."

Leo broke off, remembering.

"Go on," she whispered.

"Money didn't make any difference to Nancy when we were kids. But when I got her pregnant my freshman year in college and I had no way of supporting her, I guess Nancy got scared and thought she had to be practical."

Abby nodded. She could sympathize with an unplanned pregnancy coming as a shock and blasting a frightened girl out of her romantic dreams.

"Well, Mike, the 'gentleman' you met, was an upright, teetotaling, religious sort who never took a false step in his whole damn life. He'd been sending me to college. He'd even promised me he'd let me run his cattle operation after I graduated. When Nancy got pregnant, he kicked me off the ranch and withdrew his financial support, called me trash and worse. I told Nancy I'd marry her, but Mike convinced her I was a worthless so-and-so who'd never amount to anything without his help, so she got scared and married Cal. Now her daddy's ranch is part of theirs." His dark face tightened at the memories.

"Go on," she urged softly.

"Mike had had his eyes on Nancy's folks' ranch for a lot of years, so I guess he could look past the moral issues where she was concerned. Eventually they talked me into giving up my rights to my daughter, Julie, too. Everybody, including me, thought I'd be a bad influence on a girl." He swallowed as if he were ashamed and looked up at her.

"I think you turned out all right."

Still, he'd lost Julie. She couldn't imagine giving up her baby forever, and yet if she believed it was really the best thing for the baby… Even so, it would put her in hell for the rest of her life.

"Back then…I convinced myself it would be better for her not to be divided between two fathers, especially since I was so damned bitter."

"Maybe someday you should pursue a relationship with Julie."

His troubled gaze met hers briefly. "I have. I've always been rebuffed. She thinks I abandoned her, which is understandable, I guess."

"Maybe someday…."

"Yeah. Maybe someday. She's kind of running wild right now. Nancy and Cal got so desperate they even lowered themselves to ask me to help, but she refuses to talk to me. She says she's gotten along without me all these years, so she reckons she doesn't need me now. Hell, maybe she's right."

Abby winced. Imagining how that must hurt, she went over to the couch and sat down beside him. Her thigh touched his. Gently, she took his hand.

He threaded her fingers through his and held on tight. "We have a lot to be thankful for. Maybe we should concentrate on that," he said.

He buried his face against her neck. His breath felt warm against her skin. She took his hand and placed it on her stomach.

Holding hands while resting on her tummy, they sat together like that for a long time. He was right. She knew they should concentrate on the baby and the joy they found in each other, on their successful careers and everything else that they had to be thankful for. She must be a very spoiled person to go on moping about Becky being missing and her father being inattentive.

"You know," Leo said. "I did something crazy earlier this week, something I was ashamed of at first."

"What?"

"For years I wanted revenge on Mike Ransom. A few months ago the chance to buy his ranch cheap for the Golden Spurs fell into my lap. This week I had the papers finalized, and I forced him to come into my office to sign them. I knew taking the Running R away from him was worse than pointing a gun at his head and pulling the trigger. I thought I wanted that until he hobbled in with a cane, still blustering and trying to act tough. But he was as pale as a sheet after he picked up his pen, I got scared he was about to have a heart attack."

"What did you do?"

"I grabbed the papers and tore them in two. I told him to get the hell out of my office. He growled at me and then headed toward the door, yelling he didn't want my charity. I started remembering how patient he'd been when he'd taught me to ride as a kid, so I asked him how Julie was.

"'Wilder than Connor ever was,'" he said.

"Ransom looked so lost and desperate as he stared at me that I couldn't just let him leave, so I said, 'Why don't you sit down while I call my banker? Maybe he could help you.'

"'Don't you think I've been to bankers?' he asked.

"'Not to mine.'

"'Like I said, I don't want your charity,' he told me.'

"'You're stubborn, old man. But so am I. It would just be a loan that you'd pay back…with interest.'

"'But you'd be pulling strings to get it.'

"'Look, whether we like it or not, we're family. You're the only grandfather Julie has. I know what you've done for her. And what I haven't done. Let's just say I'm repaying an old debt.'"

Abby took his hand. "I think that's wonderful."

"I think I was a damn fool."

They say time passes quickly when you're having fun. Autumn rushed by even faster than summer had. The long, hot days with summertime cicadas gave way to cooler, crisper mornings and breezy evenings. Being pregnant, Abby was glad the heat had abated.

She couldn't get into her regular clothes any longer, and when Leo constantly touched and stroked her belly, acting like he found her expanding figure more appealing than ever, she felt beautiful and sexy and loved.

How could a man she hadn't wanted to marry make her so happy? But was he happy?

As the months passed, and her due date neared, she wondered about his feelings. Deep down, did he still feel she'd trapped him? Would those feelings surface again?

She asked him constantly if he loved her. They'd be doing chores and having a conversation about work. Or he'd be getting into his truck to drive to San Antonio and suddenly she would touch his forearm and ask, "Leo, do you love me? Do you?"

One such evening they were walking toward the porch when she interrupted him with that question. He whirled and took her in his arms. Without taking his eyes from her face, he said. "I love you. How many times do I have to say it before you'll believe me?"

"I don't know. Again and again, I guess. Forever."

"Why can't you believe me?"

"Because no one ever has loved me. A least not so that I could count on them…."

"Hell, maybe I should be the one worrying about you loving me," he said.

"Do you…worry?"

"Yeah, I do," he admitted.

"But you know I love you!"

"Do I?"

"Yes!"

"Maybe you think you do now. What if you found out something…" He stopped, his expression tensing.

"Like what?"

"Nothing." But his face was dark and haunted, and his gaze was so piercing.

"Sometimes you watch me, just like you're looking at me now," she said, feeling uneasy. "Is there something you're not telling me?"

That telltale muscle jumped in his jawline, but he said, "I like looking at you because I love you. That's all."

But his voice was too smooth.

Something really was bothering him, eating at him. She was sure of it. Too often, she was aware of him watching her, his face silent and tense. If she asked him what was wrong, he would smile or snap at her that nothing was. He would touch her stomach and kiss her and say she was beautiful and that he'd never been happier. Then it would happen again. She would catch him watching her in that way that was beginning to worry her so much.

She wanted to believe that he loved her and that they

would have a happily-ever-after life, but she'd lost everyone who'd ever loved her, so maybe she'd been damaged in some way that made her be the kind of person people left.

He went out of his way on a daily basis to be thoughtful and kind. Maybe his kindnesses and passionate responses to her at night should have reassured her. Part of her thought that she shouldn't doubt him, that by doing that maybe she would make something bad happen. And yet something lay hidden beneath the outwardly peaceful surface of their marriage. She knew he wasn't being entirely truthful.

Everyone in her life had thrown her away. She prayed with all her heart he wouldn't do it, too.

When she wasn't worrying about her marriage, she wished her father would call or come. She wanted Connor to hurry up and find Becky.

Every time she mentioned her hopes about Becky to Leo, he would tense and then watch her in that worrisome way she hated, like he was afraid. But of what? Why did talking about Becky bother him?

Often Abby wanted to be with Leo so much she carried her computer to San Antonio and worked in his office. They could take breaks together and lunch together beside the lazy, brown river under giant cypress trees. Sometimes when she had meetings she couldn't get out of in Austin, he brought his computer to her office, and Kel would set up a desk for him beside Abby's. All too often Kel would breeze inside without knocking and catch them kissing, which she loved.

In fact, Kel became disgustingly, smugly conceited about Abby's newfound connubial bliss. When she dropped Abby at the San Antonio airport to meet Leo for their flight down to the Golden Spurs for Thanksgiving, Kel couldn't resist saying something.

"Look at you," Kel said, patting Abby's tummy. "All smiles and prettily pregnant. You all are so cute, the way you kiss all the time. Didn't I tell you he was great? Can't wait to see him, can you? How long has it been—all of eight hours?"

"Seven and a half. Hey, but don't you dare act like I owe all my newfound happiness to you. Besides, who knows how long it will last?"

"Don't borrow trouble, okay?"

"It's just that... Kel, I'm so afraid that it'll all go away."

"Honey, don't be." Kel's voice was soft with compassion. Then her eyes sparkled. "Hey, who's that tall, dark guy in the Stetson over there, devouring you with his black eyes?"

"Leo!" Abby squealed, the sight of him filling her with joy and fear. Then he swooped her into his arms, and she forgot to be afraid as his hard mouth claimed hers. She loved him so very much. Putting her arms around his neck, she clung, kissing him again and again while Kel made faces at her from behind his back.

"Abby!"

Abby leapt eagerly away from the foal she and Mia had been petting. The barn doors rolled open, and the next thing she heard were Leo's boots clicking on the concrete as he kept shouting her name. Even though she enjoyed Mia's company, she'd been missing Leo all morning while he was in the ranch office, discussing business with Cole and Shanghai.

Shanghai loped into the barn after Leo just as she pushed the stall door open.

"Mia!" Shanghai shouted.

"No, it's me," Abby said. "She's in the stall brushing Angelita, who's incredibly darling."

"Most young things are," Shanghai said, "which is why the world is overpopulated."

"Kinky broke into our business meeting and said he's ready to cut the turkey," Leo said, taking Abby's hand and bringing it to his lips. "I missed you."

"You've got him besotted," Shanghai said. "His gaze kept drifting toward the barn all morning. He didn't seem the least bit interested in discussing our renovations since the fire."

Abby smiled and squeezed Leo's hand. "It's Thanksgiving. You all shouldn't be talking business."

"Ranchers don't take holidays," Shanghai said.

"Have you made any progress locating the twins?" Mia asked as she closed the stall door.

"Some," Leo said.

"Well?"

"Well—nothing. It's too soon to talk about it."

"Leo?" Abby tugged warningly at his hand. "Why the defensive tone? Mia was just asking."

"I said it's too soon. Hell, can't we forget this? We came out here because it's time for dinner, not to discuss the missing twins."

"Mia didn't mean to upset you, darling."

"I'm not upset. You were the one who said it's a holiday. So let's just forget it."

"Fine," Abby whispered, even as a chill went through her.

Those were almost the last words Leo spoke that day. Whenever anyone asked him a question during dinner, he answered with a yes or a no but didn't elaborate. He remained withdrawn on the flight back to San Antonio, barely speaking to Abby. The next morning, he got up early, even though it was Saturday, and drove to his office.

Hours later, after she'd put up their Christmas tree and decorated the house all by herself, she began to wonder if he'd be home for dinner, so she called him on his cell.

"When are you coming home?"

"When I'm done here."

"Can't you bring your work home?"

"Look—"

"Leo, is there something wrong? Something you're not telling me about?"

"I've got a lot to do, that's all. Of course, I'd rather be with you," he said.

"That's all?"

"That's all."

"Why don't I believe you?"

"I don't know. Why don't you?"

"You always get upset about the Kemble twins…."

"I get upset about a lot of other things at work, too. You just don't see me here."

"You're sure that you're not upset about anything that has to do with us?"

He hesitated a beat too long. "No, dammit. Look, I'm sorry," he whispered, sounding worried. "The last thing I want to do is upset you. I'll be home before supper. Hell, I'll be home as fast as I can get there. It's you I want, though…not supper."

When he'd showed up an hour later, he'd swept her off her feet and carried her into the bedroom, where they'd made love for hours. Later, she'd awakened in the middle of the night and had found him at the window, staring outside, his hands clenched.

Something was wrong. She knew it. But until he told her, there was nothing she could do about it.

When she tiptoed across the room and laid her hand upon his arm, he jumped.

"Problems at work?" she whispered.

"Sometimes my thoughts won't stop."

He pulled her close and kissed her hair, her lips. But even though he held her and kissed her as she lay in his arms, she felt the coiled tension in his every muscle.

"Leo?"

"I love you," he said.

Then why, oh, why, did his bleak tone communicate such despair?

The baby was due around Christmas Day, and as Christmas approached she was so huge that Leo didn't want her on the road alone. So Abby put Kel in charge and quit driving into Austin to work. Abby handled what she could for In the Pink! by phone, fax and e-mail. In her spare time she busied herself decorating the nursery and buying presents for Leo and the baby.

She and Leo had chosen not to be told the baby's sex, so she lived in a constant state of excitement wondering whether they'd have a dark-haired boy like Leo or a beautiful little girl with shining black curls. Never once did she imagine her child looking like her.

Caught up in happy thoughts about the baby, she stopped dwelling so much on her absent father or Becky or even Leo's tension. Surely whatever was bothering Leo at work would soon resolve itself.

Lizzy and Mia e-mailed her constantly, mostly concerning the baby. With every e-mail and photo of her belly that she sent them, Abby's friendship deepened with the Kemble sisters.

Leo loved her. Abby loved him. They were joyously expecting a baby.

What could possibly go wrong?

Eleven

Connor held a photograph of girl with dark golden hair closer to his webcam.

"I've got a lead on Becky. I think maybe I've found her in Albuquerque, New Mexico."

The image on Leo's screen wavered. Connor wasn't holding the picture all that steady, but from what Leo could make out, except for the shorter hair, she looked almost exactly like Abby.

His throat tightened with alarm.

"You want me to fly out there?" Connor demanded eagerly. "Or do you want me to hold off until you gut up enough to have a conversation with your wife?"

"Go!"

"Leo, if this is our girl, you're going to have to tell her."

Leo knew that already. That didn't mean he was in

the mood for brotherly wisdom, spirituality, empathy, sympathy or whatever combination Connor chose to attack him with, so he said a curt goodbye and hung up. Then he picked up the folder on his desk labeled *Caesar's daughters: Abigail, Rebecca.*

For a long time he sat at his desk, thumbing through adoption records and Connor's reports on Abby and Becky. Feeling utterly disgusted with himself, he closed the folder and pitched it back onto his desk. Then he leaned forward on his elbows, steepled his fingers and stared into space for long minutes.

He had to tell her! His hands were shaking badly. His stomach twisted. He hadn't felt this coldly afraid in years. Not since Nancy had told him she was pregnant and Old Man Ransom had thrown him off the ranch and left him penniless and helpless. Not since Cal had called him dirt and had married his girl.

Hell, he was dirt now. He should have told Abby the truth a long time ago.

He was both in love with his wife and in lust with her. He'd never thought he could be this wildly happy with any woman. Or this miserable.

On one corner of his desk sat a tiny red jewelry box with a silver ribbon. Inside was a pricey gold horse pendant encrusted with diamonds along with a gold, choker necklace that he'd bought for Abby. He'd seen the miniature horse in a shop window and had thought of Abby the first time he'd seen her riding Coco. She'd looked slim and vibrant with her dark gold hair streaming behind her. He'd known instantly that he'd had to buy the horse for Abby for Christmas.

Not that the gift gave him any joy. If he didn't tell

her that he'd known who she was, that he'd bedded her knowing it, he stood to lose everything.

But when he told her, she might turn on him again as she had after that first night. As Nancy had.

"Why can't you understand why I had to marry Cal?"

He knew too well what it was like to be out in the cold.

He cursed. How many times had he rehearsed a speech and driven home to Abby, only to decide he didn't know what to say to her. He would see Nancy's shining eyes right before all hell had broken loose. Love was not an emotion he trusted.

Damn.

He had to tell Abby. First thing, as soon as he saw her. Tonight.

When the elevator opened, Miriam glanced up, her eager smile genuine and radiant. "Hello, Mrs. Storm. You're looking…"

"Big."

"But beautiful. How do you feel?"

Abby patted her belly. "Big. Really big. Really ready."

"I'll buzz Mr. Storm and let him know you're here. He'll be so happy to see you."

"No. I want to surprise him. I thought I'd invite him to lunch. If he's busy, I'll just go shopping until he has time."

"Well, you know where his office is."

Abby was smiling as she headed down the hall.

Kel had a meeting with one of In the Pink!'s clients this afternoon in San Antonio. Abby was glad that she'd asked Kel to stop by and give her a lift to Leo's office.

"You're sickeningly in love," Kel had teased as

she'd dropped her off in front of Leo's building. "Didn't I tell you?"

"It's rude to say I told you so every single time we talk."

"But didn't I tell you so?"

"Okay. Okay. You were right about happily ever after."

Abby was still smiling as she opened the doors to Leo's private office and found herself staring across the office at his empty black leather chair. "Leo?"

He didn't answer, so she shut the doors and then went over to his gleaming desk. She couldn't help but admire how neat his desk was compared to hers. A red Christmas present with a silver ribbon and a single file folder were the only items on top of the immense expanse of polished cherry that was his desk.

After reading the tag on the gift and realizing it was for her, she picked it up and shook it. Pleased that he'd taken the time to shop for her, she set it back down. She wished it was Christmas now so that she could open it and watch him open all his presents from her. But she had to wait. The elements of surprise and loving expectancy were part of the fun of Christmas that she'd always missed. Only this year, she would have what she'd always longed for: Leo and their baby and presents, lots and lots of carefully chosen presents. As soon as the baby was born and they could travel, they'd go down to the Golden Spurs to see Lizzy and Mia.

Vaguely Abby was aware of water running in Leo's bathroom as she leaned across his desk and lifted the folder. When she saw her name on the label, she started. Curious, she was about to open the file and read it when a door opened behind her.

"Darling, I'm so glad—"

She turned and smiled at him, but instead of running into his arms, she turned back because of what she'd just read on that label.

Caesar's daughters: Abigail, Rebecca.

When her eyes met his again, he froze. He was darkly flushed, guilt staining his cheeks.

As if in a daze, Abby flipped the folder open so violently adoption papers flew out onto his desk and floor. So did several all-too-familiar photographs of herself and Becky. She picked up a picture of Becky in braids and jeans and had to fight tears because her own memories flew at her like birds of prey.

Scattered among the photographs and adoption papers were several stapled reports from Connor's security agency about the missing twins. There was a DNA report that had to do with several beer bottles Abby had drunk out of that night Leo had picked her up in the bar.

With a little cry, Abby flipped pages in one of the reports about Rebecca Collins.

She began to shake. As she read, the awful feeling dislodged from the pit of her stomach and began to slowly crawl upward until it constricted her throat and cut off her breath.

Connor had been all over Texas and Mexico looking for Becky, but Abby knew that already.

Because she'd hired him.

What she hadn't known was that Becky and she were the missing Kemble twins.

How Connor and Leo must have laughed when she'd hired Connor. Like a fool, she'd played into their hands.

"Abby…"

At the sound of Leo's voice, directly behind her now, the fist around her throat tightened. Then the sadness and horror enveloping her turned into a roaring pain ripping her heart in two. Barely able to breathe, she sagged against the desk.

Leo said, "Darling, I can explain."

Darling. How she hated him calling her that now.

He was always so cocksure and confident, he probably thought he could talk his way out of this. He probably saw her as easy and needy and malleable.

To hell with him!

His tanned face began to spin, and suddenly it wasn't his face, it was Becky's.

Wait! Wait for me!

No! Come on!

Abby was shutting her eyes against the vision of Becky when Leo said, "If you'd just listen…."

Becky vanished, and Leo's tanned face came into sharp focus, his hair as shiny and black as wet ink, his stormy, pain-filled eyes flashing as he yanked his glasses off. He was outrageously handsome.

"You don't need to. I understand everything. Just leave me alone."

Intent on escaping him, she shoved herself away from his desk and stumbled toward the tall doors. But her legs were shaky, her gait uncertain, and since he was standing only a short distance from her, he got there much faster.

When he grabbed her arms and pulled her toward the leather sofa, she was too weak to fight him.

"I was going to tell you," he said.

"Sure you were."

"Connor told me to tell you right from the first."

"Then why didn't you?"

"Because I just didn't know how."

"And when did you first know the truth?" she demanded.

"Abby…"

"When?" she said through gritted teeth. "You've got to tell me."

"A few weeks maybe…before that night in the bar."

The fist strangling her throat, her heart, her soul squeezed tighter.

"Not that I was one hundred percent sure," he said.

"Why didn't you tell me then?"

"I had to make sure."

"By screwing me?"

"I took DNA samples."

"Right. The beer bottles," she mused, more to herself than to him. "You're nothing if not efficient. Why didn't you just do your job and take the damn bottles? Why the hell did you sleep with me?"

"Be fair. Why do you think? That was as much your idea as mine! You're the one who climbed on my table and started taking off your clothes!"

"No! You be fair! You've lied to me all along! About everything! I'll bet our entire life together is a lie! You don't love me. You just wanted to marry a Kemble."

"That's not true! I do love you!"

"You want to know something—I don't believe you! I was right about you in the beginning. CEOs like you are a despicable breed. I should know because I work with them every day. You're as ruthless and ambitious as the worst of them."

"Abby, I love—"

"Shut up! You didn't like being an outsider at the Golden Spurs, did you? Somebody they could hire and fire? You wanted to be an insider, and you saw me as your ticket. You wanted it so badly that you used my pregnancy to further your career by insisting on marriage. That's the real reason you married me!"

"No."

"I can't believe how touched I was when you pretended to be so understanding about Becky."

"I'm sorry."

"I'll never believe anything you say again! Never! Did you see me weak and vulnerable and so in need of your love that you could dupe me into believing what I'd always secretly wanted to believe, that there was somebody out there who could love me?"

"No! Hell, no!"

"You knew I'd thrown myself at Shanghai, didn't you? And that he'd dumped me for Mia? You thought I was vulnerable and easy—"

"No."

"Well, we may be having a baby together, but this marriage is over! I want you and your things out of my house tonight! I'll change the locks first thing tomorrow."

"You're upset. You don't know what you're saying. I'll drive you home."

"I'm upset? Who wouldn't be? But I know exactly what I'm saying. And I mean every word of it. I'm calling Kel. She'll drive me home. Not you! And, Leo, if you're smart, you won't tell the Kembles. They're my family. Not yours. I'll tell them who I am—when I'm good and ready. I don't mean this as a threat, but you'd better be prepared for the worst. You probably won't like my version of events."

Connor's blond head filled Leo's computer screen. "You look like shit."

"Thanks."

Not sleeping, not eating and drinking half the night took their toll in a helluva hurry. Leo didn't need Connor to tell him he had to get a grip.

"So what are you going to do now?" There was no trace of any I-told-you-so superiority edging Connor's voice. He was concerned and worried.

Leo finger-combed his black hair wearily. Last night when he'd gone over to try to deliver Abby's Christmas gifts, she'd forgotten to pull her kitchen shade. He'd caught a glimpse of her through her kitchen window when she'd come to see who was on her porch.

She'd been as big as a house in her white bathrobe, but beautiful—oh, so heart-stoppingly beautiful. And sad. He'd broken her heart.

For a long moment their eyes had met and held. His breath had caught in his throat. So had hers. His pulse had raced. Then she'd snapped the shade shut, and he'd felt lost and lonely—truly horrible. Was she going to hate him forever?

He'd knocked and knocked, pounded, yelled. In the end he'd had to leave her gifts on the porch.

His life was a mess. He was a mess.

He felt sick at heart, exhausted. It had been a long, dismal week since Abby had kicked him out and changed her locks. Even if his nights were hell, he'd been trying to work during the days. Connor and he had just finished discussing Connor's report on his trip to Albuquerque. Connor hadn't found Becky after all, but he thought it wouldn't be long.

"What can I do to get Abby back?" Leo muttered. He felt lonely and pathetic. "The only way she'll communicate with me is through Kel or through her closed door. So I talk to Kel every day and yell through her door." He didn't add that he'd drunk half a fifth of scotch after he'd gone home and was still feeling the effects from the hangover.

"Keep trying. I'll pray. What about the Kembles? How are they taking the news?"

"They haven't said anything, so I don't think she's told them. But frankly, I don't care what she tells them."

"Well, that's a switch."

"All I want is Abby."

"Tell her that."

"I would…if she'd open her door or answer her damn phone."

"You dug yourself a mighty deep hole."

"I just hope to hell it isn't my grave."

"Look, I don't like the fact that you're going through this alone, but I've got too much going on to get down to the ranch anytime soon. So if you end up with nowhere to go on Christmas, you're always welcome in Houston."

Nowhere to go….

"Thanks. But I want to be near Abby, just in case. And Kel's sworn she'll let me know when Abby goes into labor."

"Okay. I've gotta go. I'd wish you a Merry Christmas. But since that doesn't seem appropriate, I'll just pray it gets merrier real fast."

"You do that."

Abby sat sipping milk in her living room. Christmas Day was dark and gray but no darker than her sorrowful mood. She kept seeing Leo's face framed by her kitchen window. He'd looked so sad and apologetic... and handsome, too. She'd wanted to touch him. To feel his body against her own.

He was a rat. An ambitious, lying, scheming rat. Determined not to think about him, she shut her eyes. Her stomach felt tight, but that was probably only because she was so big. The baby was due any day, and she felt increasingly anxious out here on her own. She was huge and unwieldy, and it wasn't easy to get up and down off the low sofa without Leo around to help her.

To hell with Leo. The last thing she needed was a man who only wanted her because she was aligned with the rich family he worked for. At least she wouldn't have to spend Christmas alone. She'd be sharing Christmas dinner with Kel's family, and Kel would be coming over later to drive her there. But that was hours away, so she had the morning all to herself.

When she finished her milk, her stomach tightened again. Gasping, she remained on the couch. She needed to wash some clothes and towels and do a few dishes, but she lacked the energy to attack the mundane chores. With her stomach muscles knotting, she felt increasingly uncomfortable, so she just sat, listening to her own breathing as the walls seemed to close in on her.

She thought about her father and then made herself

push those attachments aside. Trying not to feel sorry for herself, she bit her lower lip and stared at the mountain of gifts Leo had left for her last night and that she'd placed under their tree.

Under *her* tree.

She'd never before had so many beautifully wrapped presents, and they were all from Leo. She shouldn't have brought them in. She shouldn't have put them under her tree, but she'd never had so many presents. She hadn't been able to resist keeping them. She was especially fascinated by the small red box with the silver ribbon that she'd seen on his desk that horrible day when her fantasy world had blown up in her face. She knew it had been the last he'd purchased and couldn't help wondering what it was.

His gifts shouldn't mean anything, not now. Not when she knew the truth. His marriage had been a career move. Period.

She'd hated him that day in his office when she'd read about Becky and he'd confessed about the DNA samples. She'd vowed to hate him forever, but he'd been so sweet and attentive for so many months. And those memories haunted her. Even now he kept up his act—calling her, dropping by, sending her notes. Not that she'd answered her phone or the door. And she'd shredded all his notes without reading them. But only after clutching them to heart and nearly dying of curiosity. And yes, she was such a sap, the bits and pieces were in her lingerie drawer. The guy deserved an Oscar. He really did.

He'd made sure Coco was taken care of, and he'd ordered her to stay away from the barn until after the baby was born.

She knew his interest had to do with his ambition. No doubt he was scared as hell she'd say something to the Kembles to destroy his career. And maybe she would. It would serve him right. But every time she picked up the phone to call Lizzy and tell her what a rat Leo was, she hesitated. She couldn't forget lying in his arms after they'd made love even if she wanted to.

She closed her eyes. If only her father would call. The stillness of the house was driving her crazy. Didn't he know it was Christmas Day and that he should call?

She picked up her phone and dialed her father's cell. He didn't answer, of course, so she left another message.

"Daddy, I…I want to wish you a Merry Christmas. I sent you a gift, and I keep wondering if you got it. Where are you? Did you get any of my messages asking whether Becky and I are adopted? It's really, really important that you get back to me on that. I…I'd like to hear from you. I miss you so much. And, Daddy, I'm going to have the baby any day now. I wish…I wish that you could be here…because, Daddy, I—I left Leo…and I'm all alone. Daddy, I…I need you so much."

A robotic male voice that wasn't even a recording of her father's voice said she had thirty seconds left, so she hung up without telling him she loved him.

Daddy, why can't you be here for me…just this once?

Never had Abby felt so alone, and it was all Leo's fault. For a few brief months when he'd been with her, she'd had the illusion she was loved. He'd made her feel so complete when he'd walked in the door at night and kissed her hello and pretended he was glad to see her. Even when he'd helped her load the dishwasher, or when he'd gone to the barn to help with Coco, she'd felt he'd done those things because he'd loved her.

All of it, every precious kiss and glance and thoughtful act, even the Christmas gifts that mesmerized her, had been part of a big, calculated lie to serve Leo Storm's ruthless ambition.

He was a heartless CEO to the core.

She'd been a vulnerable, stupid, naive fool.

Well, never again!

Twelve

Abby heard Kel's knock on her front door. She was rushing to answer it, when her stomach tightened. This time the pain was so excruciating she doubled over and took several deep breaths. In the next instant, she felt something wet trickling down her leg.

Her water had broken.

Oh my God. The baby is coming.

Her first thought was of Leo. Then she hated herself for wanting him so much.

Slowly she moved toward the door, but when she opened it, Leo was actually there.

"Don't slam it," he whispered, wedging his boot inside.

He looked thinner. Last night she hadn't noticed the lines of suffering etched beneath his eyes and beside his mouth. He hadn't bothered to shave or wash his hair, and there were circles under his eyes. His T-shirt and normally creased jeans were dirt-stained and limp with sweat. He certainly didn't look like the self-confident CEO she'd married, and if he were any other human being, she would have felt compassion.

"Where's Kel?" She tried to stand up straight. She was determined to feel nothing for him even though some part of her—that weak, naive, stupid, fatherless little girl that longed to be loved—was joyously glad he was here.

"Outside," he said. "In her car. She's waiting to pick you up."

"She knows what you did and how I feel. I can't believe that she would—"

"Abby, don't be mad at her. It's Christmas. I had to see you, to make sure you're okay. She felt sorry for me and let me knock on your door."

"Well, you've seen me. I'm okay. I want you to go. Get Kel. I need—"

Her stomach tightened, and the awful pain made her squint to hold back her tears. Even so, she grabbed her belly.

"What is it?" He stepped forward, his voice rough with concern.

"Nothing," she said, but she was gasping. And he wasn't stupid.

Understanding dawned and his tanned face tensed. "It's the baby," he said softly. "How far along are the pains?"

"They're not exactly pains."

"Contractions then?"

"I haven't been timing them, but I've been having them all morning. And I think my water just broke."

"Why the hell didn't you call me?"

"You are the last person—"

"Right." Pain flashed in his eyes and was gone. "Save it," he muttered fiercely. "Do you have a bag packed?"

She nodded, suddenly glad in spite of herself that he was here and taking charge.

She'd missed him. She'd missed him so much. And she needed him.

"Abby, I know you don't believe me, but I love you. Not because you're a Kemble heiress, but because you're you. After losing Nancy and Julie, I never thought I'd get a second chance, and that makes you and the baby doubly precious."

He would have said more, but her stomach tightened painfully again. Then Kel came up behind him.

Torn, Abby bit her lips in pain.

Instantly, Leo was all business. He told Abby to get changed and ordered Kel to find fresh towels for Abby to sit on in the truck. He grabbed Abby's suitcase and something from under the tree. Then he went out and drove his truck right up to the back door.

He was an ambitious, lying rat. She'd been trying to convince herself she loathed him all week. Still, it was hard to throw a man out when he was making himself so useful.

Before she knew what was happening, he lifted her into his arms and carried her down the steps.

"I…I want Kel," she said as he opened his door and helped her climb into the cab. Not that she really wanted Kel. His arms about her felt too good.

"I'll be right behind you," Kel said, taking Abby's hand reassuringly. "Besides, I'm so nervous I might have a wreck. He's a good man," she added. "And he loves you. He's told me that every single day, and I for one believe him." She leaned closer. "Nobody's perfect,

Abby. You should know that. You've never gone out with anybody who comes close to this guy. If it was me, I'd forgive him in a heartbeat and never look back. The fact that you're a Kemble is a plus. Who knows, the guy will probably find your sister for you."

Abby didn't say anything. To his credit, once they were both buckled inside his truck, Leo simply drove. Not once did he try to defend himself again or apologize. He simply kept his eyes glued to the road and concentrated on getting them safely to Austin. Her stomach kept tightening, and every contraction hurt more than the last.

Did he love her? Maybe he wasn't perfect. But if he loved her, wouldn't that be enough? Did he have to be as perfect as some ideal husband like the guys she read about in women's magazines? Did guys who did every single thing right even exist?

The next contraction had her panting.

Vaguely she was aware of Leo's foot on the gas pedal. The pastures and houses on the outskirts of Austin whipped by. He was passing every vehicle on the road now.

She would figure it all out later. Right now they were having a baby.

Their baby.

Tucked into crisp white sheets with her black-haired son making gurgling sounds as he sucked her nipple and Leo standing proudly beside her, Abby felt serene, if a little tired.

Very tired.

Surely the happiest days are when babies are born. As long as she lived, Abby would never forget the explosion of her son's little cry or how warm and loving

Leo's dark eyes had been above his blue surgical mask. She'd felt like a queen giving birth to a prince…and like a beloved wife, as well.

To have a healthy, normal son with a man she loved. A man who loved her. Did life get much better?

"Will you ever forgive me?" Leo asked.

His eyes blazed, but his countenance was suddenly as pale as a man facing a firing squad.

"I already have. Come here, my darling."

When he moved closer, she took his big, tanned hand in hers and turned it over. Then she brought it to her cheek and held it there, needing his warmth, his strength. "I already have. I want our son to know his father."

"What about you?" he demanded huskily.

The dark pain that lingered in his voice made her heart throb.

"I never stopped loving you. I tried, but I can't. You made my life too beautiful, and I missed you too much. When I went into labor, the only thing I wanted was you with me. You make feel safe. I've never felt that way before. Not with anybody. Not even before Becky ran away."

"You damn sure had me fooled."

"I had me fooled, too."

His fingertip traced her mouth lovingly. "Oh, Abby…"

"Do you think you'll ever find my sister?"

"I'll find her…or die trying. As you know, I can be pretty ruthless when I want something. Sometimes that's a good trait. And speaking along those lines…"

When he stopped talking, she met his eyes again, only this time they were sparkling.

"Guess who's outside," he said.

"I can't imagine."

"Your father. I had Connor track him down and haul him here bodily. He was in a South American jungle in a terrorist camp, writing the story of a lifetime. But he can't wait to see you and his grandson."

"First...kiss me and hold me, Leo, my precious darling."

Leo didn't make her beg.

Very gently he leaned over the bed, careful not to mash her IV or their son. Their lips met tentatively, first in love and forgiveness and then with eagerness and desire. A long time later, he kissed the top of their son's dark head.

Then he said, "I'll get your father."

"Merry Christmas," her father said as soon as he walked into her hospital room, carrying an armload of presents.

She imagined Leo had bought the presents for him because her father had never bought a present in his life, or at least not that she knew of. But that was okay. Her father was here.

When he leaned down to kiss her cheek, he reeked of cigarettes and leather and jungle scents. His face was rough against her cheek—he needed a shave, but she didn't care. He was here at last. And all because of Leo.

"Merry Christmas, darling," Leo said as she met his gaze over her father's shoulder.

"Merry Christmas," she replied. "The first of many together...I hope."

"I promise you a lifetime of Merry Christmases," Leo said.

And she believed him.

"I can't wait to get home and open that red box with the silver ribbon," she whispered.

"You don't have to wait. I have it right here." Grinning, he pulled it out of his pocket.

When he handed it to her, she pounced on the silver ribbon with the greediness of a child who'd waited a lifetime for a real Christmas.

Her father laughed, but she cried when she saw the exquisite, diamond-studded horse.

"Coco?"

"I think I fell in love with you the first time I saw you riding her," Leo said.

Circling his neck with one arm as she cradled their son in the other, she pulled him down, and he kissed her for a very long time.

Epilogue

A throng of Kembles pressed close to Leo and his golden wife, who was standing proudly beside him as she held little Caesar Kemble Storm in her arms outside the Golden Spurs Ranch chapel. Everybody wanted a closer glimpse of the baby. Even Joanne, who'd been less than pleased when Abby's true identity had been announced.

The February day was bright and warm. Not that that was the least bit unusual in South Texas.

"Well, I guess this makes you family now," Joanne said to Leo with a slight edge in her tone.

"I guess," he replied lazily.

Mia and Lizzy had been thrilled to learn who Abby really was. While not as pleased, Joanne had not seemed surprised when Abby and Leo had gone down to the Golden Spurs for a weekend right after baby Caesar had been born to tell Lizzy and Mia who Abby really was.

But Joanne had grudgingly accepted Abby as if her presence in their family was inevitable, and she'd even congratulated Leo several times. Then, strangely, as she had at the wedding, Joanne had asked Abby about her father and hung on every word as Abby had told her about his most recent visit.

"Did he ever tell you that you were adopted?"

"Not until I asked him during his last visit. He said he'd always intended to when Becky and I were grown, but that when Becky disappeared, he couldn't face it."

"He always seemed so unafraid to me. I was the one—" She broke off.

Again Abby wondered about Joanne's intense fascination with her father.

"How did you know my father?"

"We were friends, briefly," was all Joanne had said. Abby imagined her father must have neglected her because of his work.

Now Lizzy jingled a pair of tiny spurs in front of baby Caesar's plump hands, causing Abby to forget her earlier conversation with Joanne.

"I thought baby Caesar held up pretty well for the service," Lizzy said with a big smile. "These are his, and when you all leave, I'm definitely hanging them on the Spur Tree. Right beside Daddy's."

Abby felt happier every time she was with her admiring new family and their friends. The chapel and the Big House along with all the other buildings had been freshly painted since the fire. It had rained a lot in January, and there hadn't been a freeze, so lush green grass covered most of the earth that had been black last summer.

"Baby Caesar, you were way, way better than my

Vanilla during the service," Mia said. "She's over there sulking by the barbeque pit because I am here bragging on you." Not that Mia's voice was harsh as she told stories about her lively daughter while tugging at the baby's big toe.

Baby Caesar squirmed and bit his fist as if he were drawing on the last of his reserves to be patient.

"I'm afraid I need to feed him," Abby said right before he let out an anxious little cry.

Bunching his fingers, he jammed them frantically into his mouth. When that didn't soothe him, he began to kick. Then he let out another cry.

Smoke from portable barbeque pits drifted lazily against a cloudless blue sky. Immense white tents had been put up on the back lawn to accommodate the guests, who had been invited to celebrate three new members being brought into the family.

While Mia and Lizzy had been wild to welcome Abby, the baby and Leo into the family, it was Joanne who'd suggested that baby Caesar be christened on the ranch where all family members were always christened. Of course, a christening called for a real celebration, and since they were ranchers in South Texas, a celebration called for barbeque, beer and mariachis. The musicians were setting up near the Big House.

No sooner had Abby agreed than Lizzy had overnighted Caesar Kemble's original yellowed christening gown with a note that said baby Caesar *had* to wear the founder's gown.

So here Abby was, standing by her husband as she held their wriggling baby, and surrounded by her family, too.

Finally, after everybody had gotten to pinch the baby's

toes and arms and talk baby talk to him, Leo took Abby's hand to lead her to a private parlor in the Big House where she could feed the baby before they ate lunch.

When they were alone with their baby suckling at her breast, Leo leaned down and kissed Abby long and deeply. Like all his kisses, this one promised her forever.

Without thinking, she touched the exquisite little horse with the diamond bridle at her throat that Leo had given her for Christmas. Then her hand fell to the dark, downy curls on her baby's head.

Her father was back in Argentina, and she hadn't heard from him since he'd left. Still, on the morning of his departure he'd told her how he and Electra had selected an adoption agency to arrange the adoption.

"Electra was an old friend of mine. We'd collaborated on several books. She came to me when she was pregnant, and I told her how much your mother and I wanted children. And your mother and I were so happy…for a little while—before Becky disappeared and everything went wrong."

"Yes. We were happy."

"If only…." He'd paused. "I drive myself to write, you know, so I won't think about it. I've become something of an adrenaline junkie."

"Maybe you should reach out to someone new."

"I tried that once, not so long ago. And got my heart busted up all over again. No thanks."

"I'm sorry, Daddy."

"It's okay."

Abby wasn't going to think about her father or worry about Becky right now. She had too many blessings to count. In fact, she'd never been happier as she sat in a rocking chair with her blouse unbuttoned and Caesar pressed close, her husband smiling lovingly down at her.

She couldn't have imagined such happiness. Not ever. Not in her wildest dreams.

Maybe, soon, Leo would find Becky for her and her daddy.

If any man could, Leo would.

* * * * *

Silhouette Desire kicks off 2009 with MAN OF THE MONTH, *a yearlong program featuring incredible heroes by stellar authors.*

When Navy SEAL Hunter Cabot returns home for some much-needed R & R, he discovers he's a married man. There's just one problem: he's never met his "bride."

Enjoy this sneak peek at Maureen Child's
AN OFFICER AND A MILLIONAIRE.
Available January 2009 from Silhouette Desire.

One

Hunter Cabot, Navy SEAL, had a healing bullet wound in his side, thirty days' leave and, apparently, a wife he'd never met.

On the drive into his hometown of Springville, California, he stopped for gas at Charlie Evans's service station. That's where the trouble started.

"Hunter! Man, it's good to see you! Margie didn't tell us you were coming home."

"Margie?" Hunter leaned back against the front fender of his black pickup truck and winced as his side gave a small twinge of pain. Silently then, he watched as the man he'd known since high school filled his tank.

Charlie grinned, shook his head and pumped gas. "Guess your wife was lookin' for a little 'alone' time with you, huh?"

"My—" Hunter couldn't even say the word. *Wife?* He didn't have a wife. "Look, Charlie…"

"Don't blame her, of course," his friend said with a wink as he finished up and put the gas cap back on. "You being gone all the time with the SEALs must be hard on the ol' love life."

He'd never had any complaints, Hunter thought, frowning at the man still talking a mile a minute. "What're you—"

"Bet Margie's anxious to see you. She told us all about that R & R trip you two took to Bali." Charlie's dark brown eyebrows lifted and wiggled.

"Charlie…"

"Hey, it's okay, you don't have to say a thing, man."

What the hell could he say? Hunter shook his head, paid for his gas and as he left, told himself Charlie was just losing it. Maybe the guy had been smelling gas fumes too long.

But as it turned out, it wasn't just Charlie. Stopped at a red light on Main Street, Hunter glanced out his window to smile at Mrs. Harker, his second-grade teacher who was now at least a hundred years old. In the middle of the crosswalk, the old lady stopped and shouted, "Hunter Cabot, you've got yourself a wonderful wife. I hope you appreciate her."

Scowling now, he only nodded at the old woman—the only teacher who'd ever scared the crap out of him. What the hell was going on here? Was everyone but him nuts?

His temper beginning to boil, he put up with a few more comments about his "wife" on the drive through town before finally pulling into the wide, circular drive leading to the Cabot mansion. Hunter didn't have a clue what was going on, but he planned to get to the bottom of it. Fast.

He grabbed his duffel bag, stalked into the house and paid no attention to the housekeeper, who ran at him, fluttering both hands. "Mr. Hunter!"

"Sorry, Sophie," he called out over his shoulder as he took the stairs two at a time. "Need a shower, then we'll talk."

He marched down the long, carpeted hallway to the rooms that were always kept ready for him. In his suite, Hunter tossed the duffel down and stopped dead. The shower in his bathroom was running. His *wife?*

Anger and curiosity boiled in his gut, creating a churning mass that had him moving forward without even thinking about it. He opened the bathroom door to a wall of steam and the sound of a woman singing— off-key. Margie, no doubt.

Well, if she was his wife… Hunter walked across the room, yanked the shower door open and stared in at a curvy, naked, temptingly wet woman.

She whirled to face him, slapping her arms across her naked body while she gave a short, terrified scream.

Hunter smiled. "Hi, honey. I'm home."

* * * * *

Be sure to look for
AN OFFICER AND A MILLIONAIRE
by USA TODAY *bestselling author Maureen Child.*
Available January 2009 from Silhouette Desire.

CELEBRATE
60 YEARS
OF PURE READING PLEASURE
WITH **HARLEQUIN**®!

We'll be spotlighting a different series
every month throughout 2009
to celebrate our 60th anniversary.
Look for Silhouette Desire® in January!

Collect all 12 books in the Silhouette Desire®
Man of the Month continuity, starting in
January 2009 with *An Officer and a Millionaire*
by *USA TODAY* bestselling author
Maureen Child.

Look for one new Man of the Month title
every month in 2009!

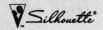

SPECIAL EDITION™

**The Bravos meet the Jones Gang
as two of Christine Rimmer's famous
Special Edition families come together
in one very special book.**

THE STRANGER
AND TESSA JONES
by
CHRISTINE RIMMER

Snowed in with an amnesiac stranger during a
freak blizzard, Tessa Jones soon finds out her
guest is none other than heartbreaker Ash Bravo.
And that's when things really heat up....

*Available January 2009
wherever you buy books.*

REQUEST YOUR FREE BOOKS!

2 FREE NOVELS PLUS 2 FREE GIFTS!

Passionate, Powerful, Provocative!

YES! Please send me 2 FREE Silhouette Desire® novels and my 2 FREE gifts (gifts are worth about $10). After receiving them, if I don't wish to receive any more books, I can return the shipping statement marked "cancel". If I don't cancel, I will receive 6 brand-new novels every month and be billed just $4.05 per book in the U.S. or $4.74 per book in Canada, plus 25¢ shipping and handling per book and applicable taxes, if any*. That's a savings of almost 15% off the cover price! I understand that accepting the 2 free books and gifts places me under no obligation to buy anything. I can always return a shipment and cancel at any time. Even if I never buy another book, the two free books and gifts are mine to keep forever.   225 SDN ERVX 326 SDN ERVM

Name	(PLEASE PRINT)	
Address		Apt. #
City	State/Prov.	Zip/Postal Code

Signature (if under 18, a parent or guardian must sign)

Mail to the **Silhouette Reader Service:**
IN U.S.A.: P.O. Box 1867, Buffalo, NY 14240-1867
IN CANADA: P.O. Box 609, Fort Erie, Ontario L2A 5X3
Not valid to current subscribers of Silhouette Desire books.

Want to try two free books from another line?
Call 1-800-873-8635 or visit www.morefreebooks.com.

* Terms and prices subject to change without notice. N.Y. residents add applicable sales tax. Canadian residents will be charged applicable provincial taxes and GST. Offer not valid in Quebec. This offer is limited to one order per household. All orders subject to approval. Credit or debit balances in a customer's account(s) may be offset by any other outstanding balance owed by or to the customer. Please allow 4 to 6 weeks for delivery. Offer available while quantities last.

Your Privacy: Silhouette Books is committed to protecting your privacy. Our Privacy Policy is available online at www.eHarlequin.com or upon request from the Reader Service. From time to time we make our lists of customers available to reputable third parties who may have a product or service of interest to you. If you would prefer we not share your name and address, please check here.

SDES08R

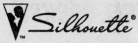

COMING NEXT MONTH

#1915 AN OFFICER AND A MILLIONAIRE—
Maureen Child
Man of the Month
A naval officer returns home to discover he's married…to a woman he's never even met!

#1916 BLACKMAILED INTO A FAKE ENGAGEMENT—
Leanne Banks
The Hudsons of Beverly Hills
It started as a PR diversion, but soon their pretend engagement leads to real passion. Could their Hollywood tabloid stunt actually turn into true love?

#1917 THE EXECUTIVE'S VALENTINE SEDUCTION—
Merline Lovelace
Holidays Abroad
Determined to atone for past sins, he would enter into a marriage of convenience and leave his new wife set for life. But a romantic Valentine's Day in Spain could change his plans.…

#1918 MAN FROM STALLION COUNTRY—
Annette Broadrick
The Crenshaws of Texas
A forbidden passion throws a couple into the ultimate struggle—between life and love.

#1919 THE DUKE'S BOARDROOM AFFAIR—
Michelle Celmer
Royal Seductions
This charming, handsome duke had never met a woman he couldn't seduce—until now. Though his new assistant sees right through him, he's made it his business to get her into his bed!

#1920 THE TYCOON'S PREGNANT MISTRESS—
Maya Banks
The Anetakis Tycoons
Months after tossing his mistress out of his life, he discovers she has amnesia—and is pregnant with his child! Pretending they're engaged, he strives to gain her love *before* she remembers.…

SDCNMBPA1208